Eternal Essence of Being

The Measure of Enough

Dezera R.B. Davis

author@dezeradavis.com

Ordering Information:
Quantity sales. Special discounts are available on quantity purchases by corporations, associations, and others. For details, contact the publisher at the email address above.

Printed in the United States of America
Publisher's Cataloging-in-Publication data
Davis, Dezera R.B.
Eternal Essence of Being : The Measure of Enough / Dezera R. B. Davis.
231p. cm.
ISBN 9781517397487
1. Fiction 2. 1970s Theme 3. African-American Literature
First Edition
14 13 12 11 10 / 10 9 8 7 6 5 4 3 2 1

I would like to thank my family for their support throughout this journey to publication.

Extra special thanks to the one who has always inspired us to be creative –

My Mom, Dr. Beulah (Goines)

A Very Special Dedication to My Uncles,

Who Mean So Much to Me:

To Uncle Henry L., who would probably have taken a really nice
Polaroid.

To Uncle R. E. Jr., who would hopefully have stood up and folded
his arms, which indicates the ultimate in approval.

To Uncle Joey, who would have said "Deza, what is this?" And then
I'd find out from Mommy that he proudly told ALL of Unit 4 School
District that his niece wrote a book.

And To Uncle T-Bone, I'm grateful I can still just call you and ask...
I'll Jitterbug at your Hop! Love you, Deza

"So, you want in?" Are you gonna want to go? Oh, please, yes, yes, yes!" Kary Parsons, drama times ten, but, very wonderfully so. Kary, about two inches from the tip of my nose. Kary who has a way of coming ever so close into the realm that violates one's personal space, air space, line of sight, and breathing room. Kary, who at this moment fancied the chic Bobbed hairstyle of the Twenties, and in every moment, the Abe of the 70's.

My name is Abe. I am a writer, and bi-monthly member of the Eden Club writers group; bi-monthly as in questionable, as to whether my accommodations have been paid for the month. I'm not poor, by any stretch. I just don't always plan my resources very well. However, that is on par for the majority of the Eden Club writer's group members. Our attendance averages an eight-person group at any given time. Part of our poorly allocated resources include the fully stocked Eden bar. So management tolerates our temperamental group including the cast of characters that may, at any given time, be center stage in the atrium we covet at the end of the bar, and our occasional arrears. Yes, the Eden Club and the writer's group were my paradise, my world, all that I wanted to imagine, all that I could live. It should have been enough.

Kary Parsons: persistent, hopeful, feminine, determined. Kary reminded me of a dandelion. Pretty, bright at her peak, but wispy and transparent at her core. One dismissive wind and it's on to the next big thing. Kary joined the Eden Club writers group about three years ago. I founded the group out of the desperate need to get away from the heady political writing and laborious social commentary of the day. I wanted fun, imaginative, playful, and adventurous; poets and novelists need only apply.

The penetrating stare of deep emerald found its mark and bore in deep, I gave in.

"Kary, what is it?"

I had long since lost the ability to tell her no. Nevertheless, I held steadfastly to my inquiries and demand for details; itinerary and the sort. Squeak, squeal and squawk with glee, she was all too happy to indulge.

"Only the best ever, the re-opening and dedication of Cornerstone Resort, the premiere relaxation destination for the soul vacation."

"I take it you are the illustrious composer of that little ditty." I smiled.

Kary's contribution to the world of literature generally consisted of promotion and marketing for high end resorts, social events and all things on the calendar of society's elite. She also supplemented her income by writing for various women's lifestyle magazines.

"People pay me for my opinion Abe".

Apparently my deadpan expression and sarcastic tone translated in Kary-speak as "please continue with much zest, zeal, and gusto". Which translated into Abe-speak as "I'm gonna need another whiskey".

Emitting a slight humph at the brief delay, she continued. "Just look at the brochure and decide for yourself. It will also help me determine if my advertising schlock is effective. Does it make you just want to free your soul, lose control, and be in the know?"

No, but it is Kary Parsons. So yes, I accepted the brochure with a smile, duly noting the snorts and empathetic head-shaking from our fellow attendees. Yeah, there were other people in the room. But from a purely observational and all-up-in-my-space standpoint: shapely legs, athletic curves, creamy skin, emerald eyes and naturally curly hair, that was usually, waxed, weaved or wigged, all packaged up into a bouncing, shoulder shimmying package. Kary Parsons had a way of making you forget to note the details of your environment, or something along those lines.

This evening's group was small. We were six in total. We could more than accommodate the fifteen members when all were present. The Atrium was called Eden, leading to the not so terribly ingenious name of the group, especially considering the shit load of talent we possessed. It was beautifully decorated. The owner's wife was a horticulturist in a past life. Eden was filled with the most exotic plants and the tall ceiling more than fit the ample array of transplanted trees and vines. Roses, pansies, lilies, and orchids contributed to a virtual greenhouse, which was a thorough enough explanation of paradise for us, and the ungodly amount of chilled libations consumed in the vicinity. Tonight we would be discussing Neil Crater's latest offering. He was working on a movie script. A little violent for my taste, but a nice step away from the ghetto hero themed movies currently dominating the scene. He was hyped about working with a new director he met during grad school, and together they would "change the face of cinema". His words not mine. I believed in Neil, if for nothing else but his sheer determination and diligence. He was the one member who showed every week with new content, revised story lines, and generally work done.

I ordered another round of cocktails and we discussed how ready audiences were for new formats, camera angles, and stories within a story. Exactly how much back history should one share about a character? Does a hero need to be developed beyond the heroism? Most of us wrote novels, poems, and contemporary pieces: real Hollywood entertainment writing was reserved for dreaming and scheming. However, it was always fun to discuss as if we really had a chance, a say; an opportunity to make a contribution versus the "difference" lingo of the day. Under Kary's lingering eye, I realized the Cornerstone Resort request was not going to go away. I dare not leave the matter unattended, lest her imagination get the better of her sanity.

As the evening began to wind down, our minds stimulated, spirits warmed and the essence of Eden alive in us all, I turned my full attention to Kary. She sipped the last remains of her vodka martini, licked the corners of her mouth left, right, and done.

Deep swallow. I asked her to tell me more about Cornerstone Resort.

"Cornerstone has been around forever. It used to be one of those campy resorts where they taught ballroom dancing and crafts as part of the regularly scheduled programming. Where the rich could go and come home talking about swimming holes and fishing poles without all the mud and muck of the poor. They would have the customary big dance at the end of the season and summer love and blah-be-whosee. But now…"

Kary was never one to linger on lesser points.

"With the re-opening Abe, there is going to be a casino, an actual dance club, not just a dance room or floor. There'll be restaurants, as in multiple places to dine. Oh Abe, the grounds are being redone. They're adding suites and villas. And it's going to be so Hollywood. You can dress up or down, lounge by the pool, party 'til dawn, and…"

I had to interrupt, again the whole imagination versus sanity thing. I did love to see her green eyes sparkle with excitement. She created her own energy and her light auburn hair wisped in the airy breeze around her, caused by her easy sway as she talked. Kary's life and light was the essence of Eden Club. It should have been enough.

"Kary, Kary!!! Let me think about it. I will read the brochure tonight, I promise."

And I meant it. Nothing compliments neat bourbon like a little light reading material and a warm fire. My reward: a squeak, squeal, squawk, and million dollar grin. I was taking the bait.

We rounded out the evening with club business, dues and good cheer. We said our goodnights, and parted as always, as friends. I headed weary and slightly wobbly to my room. I placed an order with room service; a burger, fries, and milkshake to be sent to my room. I had a small two-room suite, room 419 at the Hotel Selvyn.

The Eden Club writers group met weekly in the bar atrium on the lower level. By special arrangement and a nominal fee, I'd maintained my room there for four years now. I moved in just after finishing graduate school, at the end of the summer. With coastal Carolina becoming more of a tourist destination than a status designation, my parents retired to the Virgin Islands and rented out the family home. I had ninety days to vacate. So, I landed here, and the "special arrangement" with Hotel Selvyn management? My weekly writer's group; they spend enough on drinks, dinners and guests to make it advantageous to keep us, well me, around.

Plus I work part-time, as needed, in the office assisting with various media communication essentials, and Ivan Selvyn was a friend of my dad's. Probably should have led with that ditty. I also had a modest income from various writing and photojournalism opportunities. I was still close with a small group of grad school friends who worked various media outlets, local news stations and a couple of prestigious magazines, *Time* and *National Geographic*. I contributed mostly stateside pieces. I was a good photographer and could pinch hit a respectable human interest article in crunch-time.

The Selvyn chef was first class, his meals a symphony; the burgers gourmet; the fries crispy, both white and sweet potato, with a French cut; and last but not least, the delicious proprietary sorbet milkshakes. I let my dinner digest as I looked out the window across the city. Downtown lights danced against the night dew creating a dream-like sequence on the concrete sidewalks. I should walk off the meal, but the low plush recliner in the living room section of my suite beckoned. The wrinkles in the dark leather appeared to wink like an aged but tawdry temptress, promising to treat my body in a manner only time and experience could grant; contoured to fit, my lazy day mistress. I succumbed. I awoke abruptly around midnight to clamoring down the hall. Party revelers in full regalia ready for the sweet funk only The City of New York can promise on a Tuesday night.

I begin to think about the peacefulness of a free spirit, unbound joy, unencumbered relaxation and indulgence, a soul vacation: Cornerstone. Remembering the details of Kary's description earlier, the girl had a knack for mixing eloquence and rabblerousing into one glorious and salacious package. She started with the reminiscence only childhood memories produce; Cornerstone Resort Homes, its former name. A place where fathers leave their briefcases in the lobby and mothers become women. Endless freedom, exploration, genuine laughter, and decadence unhindered; no explanations for high expectations, ridiculous wealth, uninhibited spending, and no excuses or apologies for being the empirical elite.

I thought about the new Cornerstone, where the next generation would build their memories of young adulthood. Spend their money or trust funds, define the decadence of the era, and breathe life into the cold limestone building and marble floors. Illuminate the lobby and halls with the shimmer and shine of sequins and diamonds, scuff the floors with polished platforms, and set the heartbeat of the once quiet countryside to a pulse that would determine the standard for the new playgrounds for the rich and famous. I raised my whiskey-filled glass to Kary Parsons and her Cornerstone: "Yes, I want in!"

I sent out a formal letter to the Eden Club members, all total fifteen when everyone was accounted for, informing them that next month's meetings would be canceled. All four weeks. I would visit Cornerstone, as Kary's guest for the thirty-day 'Playa's Stay'.

Another one of Kary's marketing genius SoundBits; it sounded good rolling off the tongues of the late night deejays on the "all funk, all the time" stations taking over the airwaves.

Dear esteemed Eden Club members,

As club founder and President, I am writing to inform you that the May series of meetings have been canceled. Our meeting Friday will be the last until the first Tuesday in June. I have accepted an illustrious invitation to attend the Grand Re-opening and dedication of the Cornerstone Resort in Michigan.

I look forward to the illuminating experience and will return to regale you with tales of adventure, excitement, and marvels of the new venue. Polaroids and antidotes will abound. Until then, fair well, write well, and drink well. And if you must while I'm away, marry well. Someone's got to pay our tab!!!

Peace, Love and Literature

The Friday meeting was full of prose, toasts, well wishes and good man's (for the long train ride with Kary's delightfully endless chatter, tongue heavily piercing cheek). Kary was decidedly absent from the farewell send off. Home, I imagined, frantically packing, posing and pouting. Trying to gather only the most fabulous of attire, akin to the Ms. America competition, swimwear, evening wear, opening number, entertainment, interview and numerous other categories as yet defined, established or chartered for that matter. By evening's close it had been unanimously voted to continue with the weekly meetings for discussion purposes. More likely idle gossip, speculation, and commentary on Cornerstone happenings; not necessarily a stifle to creativity amidst writers and the sort, and hardly needing my correspondence, input or explanation.

I arrived at Penn Station in record time, having chosen a cabbie alternative to the subway. Being writers and wanting to take advantage of the wonderful views of landscape and inspiration, Kary and I opted for the newly formed Amtrak Rails. I agreed to meet Kary in the Lounge Car where we could absorb the experience in its entirety with the usual accouterments, cocktails and cigarettes. I received a note at the Hotel Selvyn front desk informing me that Kary would meet me at the next station stop due to unforeseen delays with last minute copy promoting the Cornerstone trip. She could be a perfectionist when need be. I knew she had fond memories of Cornerstone and recounting the past and selling the future were of equal priority for excellence. I would later reflect with gratitude on the chance to relax alone and take in the travelers, and departing sights and sounds of the New York platform.

I settled comfortably into the Lounge car as I awaited the train departure. As I closed my eyes, a sharp sound pierced my ear. I briefly thought the accompanying scratching sandpaper sound was the friction of the rails and wheels. Only to open my eyes and find a harried middle aged woman, inches from my ear, requesting the seat next to me, at what I can only determine was the top of her lungs. I am certain for the sake of all things vocal, she did not need the small cigar she lit frantically.

By nature of being a relatively silent observer, I tend to collect unsolicited conversation and dialogue. Case in point, the seemingly harried woman, whose identity and a few more unsolicited tidbits were soon to become known to me, sandpapered her way into my being.

"Mah' nerves are just awful. The trains, the people, where are they going, really on a Saturday mahrning? What requires them?"

She inhaled deeply, which by last accounts you do not do with a cigar; further support in explanation of the rusty screeching sandpaper sound.

"Bertha, (she introduced herself), nice to meet ya' kid. Whar ya headed?"

She nestled in and hunkered down. I cleared my throat with a so-this-is-happening reply.

"Uh, just out to a resort vacation thing with a friend." Little detail as possible Abe, we got a talker.

"Oh, one of those." She pursed her lips pensively through a smoky haze. Her eyes roved over me with a way in which I thought only Kodak Instamatic had a patent. "You don't look the type."

'The Type'. Okay, so admittedly, curiosity sparked. "What type might that be Bertha?"

She gave a puff, shrug, "Oh you know, the resort type. But you, kid, you got that creature comfort vibe to me. Whereas I, on the other hand, been resortin' for years. Someone's gotta pay for all this."

She pushed up her sizable bosom and motioned towards her body; packed tightly in a leopard print jumpsuit that in the concrete jungle surely distinguished her as leader of the pack. She accessorized with gold bangles, platform mules of indiscernible animal prints, and red lipstick that gave the distinctive look of having just devoured someone's young. And, if the scarf wrapped loosely around the mess of dark brown and golden blonde curls and wooden spike earrings were any indication, a small tribal village was anxiously awaiting the return of their warrior queen. I lit a cigarette just to keep up. The striking of the flint in the lighter help to drown the sandpaper "Ha-Ha" that spontaneously erupted from her.

Awkward smiles all around; nonetheless, with Bertha in what I can only imagine was the beginning of "full swing", I sipped my beverage in mental solitude and listened.

"So where you headed sweetheart?"

I thought, what the hell, give it up and she might go away. "Cornerstone. Cornerstone Resort in Michigan." I replied as flatly as possible.

Bertha delivered a wide wicked slap to my chest. "No kidding (screeecch), me too sugar. They called back ol' Bertha Mack; a one night only kinda deal."

"Oh, (damn my curiosity…said it with just a hint too much of interest and Bertha was clearly all about too much. Now I gotta follow through. "You're an entertainer?"

"Kid, when you come in this package, you're always entertainment (insert sandpaper ha-ha). Honey, I used to be a hostess, cigarette girl, cabaret singer, and all around party filler. They're doing an old Hollywood glamour night and asked some of us girls back. I am obviously fulfilling the glamour requirement (screech, sandpaper, screech). Anyway sweetie, can I get one of those?" She gestured towards my open pack of smokes.

I would have given her the whole pack if it meant she'd go away. Instead I slide out one for her and get a fresh one out for myself. Bertha was right, the package was downright entertainment and the train had another thirty minutes before pulling out of the station. Bertha regaled me with tales of Cornerstone according to the working class as we worked our way through a few more cigarettes and a few whiskey sours each, before she headed off to sleep in her own car. The train rumbled to life and my mind wandered.

Bertha had shared her Cornerstone with me. The themed nights, plays, dances, and entertainers; a time when the only color that mattered was green, a brief moment in the Cornerstone (Resort Homes) history. The owners at the time were rumored to be descendents of slaves, escaped to Canada for freedom. They let everything pass at Cornerstone, including themselves. Bertha, like the lines in her face, told a story of glamour and beauty and acceptance, a short lived heyday. But, maybe all things can be revived, restored to a thing of beauty, even for a one night only kinda deal.

I closed my eyes and thought of the Eden Club. Already had a story to tell and I knew Harrison and Harlow, our resident historians, would weave a glorious best-seller out of Bertha's alone. That was the beauty and grace of the Eden Club members. We wrote the stories. We told the tales. We created the legends and worlds, and they were majestic. Places filled with turmoil, chaos, discourse, love, lives. We could weave, build, destroy or guide by merely thinking them into existence. Writing it made it so. We put the words to paper, and in the minds of our readers, we were next to Gods.

The train hiccupped slightly as the Conductor announced our departure and arrivals. By being in one of the last cars, I was able to watch the train as it snaked around the curved track, carrying a full load of hopeful travelers to our next destination. As we rode through the city, I could see the tall rooftop of the atrium of Eden, hinting at the lushness inside. Finally able to relax and needing to follow the sour with sweet, I took out a slice of the Dutch apple pie which the Selvyn chef had prepared for my farewell dinner; Chef's homage to my curiosity taking me from the Big Apple to the Dutch country of Michigan. I bit slowly into the crisp buttery crust and thick filling. Swallowing the last bite of apple, I focused my thoughts on the new Cornerstone as sight of Eden slipped slowly out of view.

My resting body swayed with the gentle rocking of the rail car. The whiskey and pie had done their job well. I must have dozed off for a good hour or more when I heard soft, kid-ish laughter, felt a warm breeze in my ear and inhaled the scent of white musk and jasmine; without even opening my eyes…Kary Parsons.

"You made it." I mumbled, only half awake.

"I wouldn't miss this for the world, and you know it Abe."

I turned my head and opened my eyes to see Kary Parsons dolled up in her Furstenberg finest, the newest, latest and greatest must have Diane Von Furstenberg Wrap Dress. Kary's was a cream and brown print, and accessorized with bold, chunky gold pieces. Her outfit could have paid for six months at the Selvyn easy, especially if you count the shoes, no doubt. And not at my friends of family rate. She was all smiles; classic, pretty, shiny Kary. I sat up, stretched, and took it all in. She had traded her Bob hairstyle for, well…

"Nice hair Farrah." I smirked.

"Ass! It looks good on me!" Kary fired back.

"So that's why you had to tell me." I laughed heartily, as did she.

It did look good on her though. She took out a cigarette as she hailed the passing Porter and requested a Tom Collins on the rocks. The cigarette surprised me, as it was a general consensus among the Eden Club members that Kary talked way too much to be bothered with blowing smoke. Quiet Kary, means stay woke Abe.

I could sense her uneasiness, a rare moment that as a friend requires direct attention. "So, what's up? All jazzed for the big home coming?" Kary took a long drag on her cigarette and blew the smoke slow and cool through her nostrils.

"It ain't Eden Club Abe," was all she said.

I took her hand in mine and flashed one of her million dollar grins at her. "I know." I squeezed her soft hand tightly, until I drifted off to sleep.

We both napped briefly, fallen victims to the gently rocking of the rail car. We awoke with the conductor announcing meal service in the dining car. Unwilling to give up prime seating in the lounge car we took turns going to the dining car to quickly take out sandwiches. I, being a gentleman, would have gone for us both, but I've known Kary long enough to know I'd never get it exactly right. We chatted politely with other loungers, laughing amongst ourselves at the abominable number of boldly colored leisure suits that passed our line of sight. Even rainbows have a limited number of colors visible to the naked eye. Kary noted too, that the pot of gold was customarily at the end of the rainbow, not the front of the mouth. But we digress, and their destination was more of the Michigan City variety. No worries.

Bellies full of deli sandwiches and kettle chips, we opted for the observation deck to nurse our drinks for the evening. Since we didn't go for the full dining car deal, we had our pick of seats in the glass covered car. The evening sun was just beginning to set, so the sky was a painted masterpiece. Had we poets from our little group present, we would have never gotten them back. It was an unusually quiet ride with Kary, so I waited patiently for her moment.

Surprisingly, the break in the silence startled me.

"You know Abester…"

Quick with the interrupt, "Kary, it's not gonna take. Jeez." (I gave a sigout expression, my own portmanteau of sigh/pout, probably not going to take either, huh).

Abe…I'm excited about you meeting the crew."

Watching my face closely, she hesitated. And there it was. Lest the silence have gone unexplained. Kary knew I loathed surprise beginnings. Had I known there was a "crew" this trip would have been one fewer.

"Son of a bitch, seriously Kary?" In these cases, it's just rude not to express your displeasure.

"It's not like that Abe. They're not like, anything, like what you're thinking. They aren't stuffy, or fluffy or icky or… Well, they are a real group, real friends, fun, witty, smart, oh a real sort Abe." When she started talking bunny and Gidget at the same time, I had to give her a chance. I promised her the college-educated analytical observer side of me would dominate and I would refrain from judgment, predisposition, and stereotyping, for the moment. However, the need-another-whiskey side of me had his doubts. This was Cornerstone. The grout holding the brick together was made of paste from old money. The closest I had come to the Old Cornerstone was a college professor telling me that unless I was changing my major from Literature to Social Anthropology and writing my master's thesis on the Caste Systems of America, my summer internship would be better spent at Space Camp before going there. Nuff said!

The stillness of the night, the hum of the rails and the attentive Porter made for a pleasant, reflective, and humbled Abe. I chatted with

Kary about all the renovations and changes that birthed Cornerstone Resort, taking it from mere mild-mannered housewife to the bejeweled chanteuse of the Midwest. It was rumored the whole future resort site was literally shrouded in mystery until this very night. Dramatic Kary. The glint in her green eyes rivaled even the finest emerald. That million dollar grin lasted the rest of the train ride, until her sparkling white teeth were swallowed whole by the slowly forming steady smile that graced her face as the conductor announced the arrival at our final destination: South Haven, Michigan. She looked at me and winked. Squeak, Squeal, Squawk, I had taken the bait.

It was glitz, glam, and smile for the camera man from the moment we stepped off the train. Kary, fancying herself a roving reporter, knew how to evade, elude, and evacuate the mob scene, as we were quickly ushered into one of a long line of what could only be explained as All Terrain Vehicle Limousines. The first and only hint of the 'catch what you eat' rural Michigan I had previously imagined.

As we settled into the plush leather seats, I asked only slightly sarcastically "Over the top much?"

Grinning, Kary giddily replied, "You ain't seen nothing yet, man."

We were whisked away on a fifteen mile trek of pure sand and beach, an applicable case for the ATV-Limos. As we neared our beach spot destination, my heart slowly sank for Kary. It looked like we were arriving at a boat docking area or rather a yacht sales yard; no huge resort megaplex, just a sea of large white beasts. But as the cool night air cleared my whiskey shot eyes, I saw the blinding sea of running lights, and felt the breeze of crest flying flags. I clenched at the piercing yelps, yowls, and whoo-hoos that only the worry free, this is how it be, very rich and very poor can harbor – their singular common trait – foreign to the ears of the trailing, Jones'-Hungry, nail-biting middle classes.

I looked on in be-mazement (yup, that's staying right where it is), as she leapt eagerly from the still slowing ATV Limo. So much for the heart-sinking condolences and anticipation of the safe, quiet, and reflective ride back to the calm of Eden.

I guess I should have read the fine print. It would have been enough. The opening ceremony and dedication would take place at 5:00 PM the following evening, with the grand unveiling of Cornerstone Resort. The pre-opening festivities were to take place on private yachts floating gently on Lake Michigan. Apparently, this was a BYOY party (Bring Your Own Yacht), a Yacht Hop style meet-and-greet for the hardcore enthusiast of all things decadent.

Unsure of where to go next, and having long since lost track of my baggage (if only the hotels and private transport in New York operated on the "tip is implied", as it appears to be at Cornerstone. I'm no newbie. It's all on the back end somewhere, maybe the indents in my thumb and index finger will fade during the stay), I followed closely on Kary's well-heeled ass.

We trekked as glamorously as the soft sand would allow; when erupting from Kary came, Squeal, Squeak, Squawk times ten!

I looked up to see the motive for the commotion. A man in a slightly leaning Captain's Hat, or, a slightly leaning man in a Captain's Hat who hollered back, "KARY PARSONS!" Yup, that was the top of his lungs.

As Kary hurried up the platform, eager and excited, she made brisk introductions.

"PETER!!!!! Oh Abe, this is us! Oh Peter, this is Abe."

Peter, aka man in the slightly leaning Captain's Hat or slightly leaning man in the Captain's Hat, dutifully responded. "Alas, good man. Any friend of Kary's is a friend of mine that needs a drink. What'll it be? Nyla!!! Again, full lung capacity.

"KARY!!!!" The pitch perfect greeting delivered with ear piercing accuracy belonged to the aforementioned Nyla.

Kary jumped for joy and ran straight into the waiting, wafting figure on deck, "Nyla, Darling", Squeal, Squeak, Squawk the B side!!!!

The lovely and omnificent Nyla turned to me. "You must be Abe. You're going to have to raise your alcohol content if you want to be top shelf, what can I get you?"

"Whiskey, straight."

"We don't judge, Abe." She smiled and winked over her shoulder.

Peter ushered me further on deck as we followed the ladies inside. "You all will be our guests for the night, think of this as home base. Mi Yacht is Su Yacht. So you had better drink a lot, and I'm off to do my P-art!" With Oh-lay arms, he was indeed off.

Kary turned to me and smiled. A Million Dollars!

I surveyed my surroundings. The cherry wood and brass interior was magnificent. Plush leather sectional seating, floating candles in crystal bowls on hand-carved end tables contrasting the bright lights of the bar, added to the ambiance. Lights dancing off the bottles creating a multi-faceted stream of dancing colors more majestic than the Studio 54 disco balls. Top Shelf in no time at all.

Kary had long since disappeared in the dizzying stream of well-wishers and party starters that hopped from Yacht to Yacht. I, for the moment, felt a little more comfortable at home base.

Nyla and her husband Peter were Bogie and Bacall at their finest. She was pretty, defiantly sexy. Her deep, husky voice made me most agreeable to the dark libations that ensured my glass never held a breeze. He was suave. Welcoming in a don't-shit-where-you-eat kind of way; an everyman; if every man were a millionaire.

Between the sea of bodies and motion of the sea, I thought a walk and cool breeze might be a nice set up to the second wave. I overheard one of the revelers announce the late comers. I was not sure the gauge, since there was no clear beginning or end to the celebration.

As I walked along the beach, more than happy to blame the shifting sand on the weaving pattern of my footsteps, I caught only a glimpse of a long black yacht pulling into the harbor. Eyeing, the sleek and shiny form in the myriad of lights bobbing from yacht to yacht, it was as the lighthouse beacon swept the horizon, I saw for a brief moment the unmistakable, custom made, red, black, and green flag swaying in the wind…Uncle Roscoe had arrived.

Uncle Roscoe was one well-rounded cat. He had long since broken the yoke of proper society. Kind of like I want to be, but am not yet quite brave enough to do. Roscoe gets his full props from the Player's Club, but I still need those Diner's Club credentials. Uncle was more gin on the rocks, teal suit and zebra print Stacy Adams with baby blue soles than genteel. My grands had long since left Roscoe unspoken, choosing instead to focus all their efforts on my mom. My mom, who embraced all the old Southern values, including marrying well. Her most rebellious act being that daddy's old money was from the islands, not the mainland, still rich black soil nonetheless. At any rate it was always nice to see family, even if in the most unlikely of places. Roscoe and Cornerstone – I had to wonder – what's the catch?

I had limited options: home base or familial obligation. Damn, the shortest distance between two bottles is a straight shot. And since Uncle Roscoe just arrived, he was more likely to have two full bottles. I set out towards Uncle Roscoe's Yacht, the Night Owl

(*Cause Money Don't Sleep*. His words not mine).

Aboard the Night Owl the interior was in direct and stark contrast to

the cherry wood and brass of home base. I am not even sure where

you find Cheetah Fur paneling and wall to wall bear skin carpeting.

But Uncle Roscoe did, and in no short supply.

"Nephew!!! Welcome and come well, let my ladies get us

something to sip on. Ladies, this is my Nephew Abe. Abe meet

Champagne and Caviar, one cause' she bubbly, and the other cause a

rich man don't eat Tuna." *Classic Roscoe.*

"Uncle Roscoe!" If I squeak, squealed, and squawked, I

would have for my favorite Uncle. Uncle Roscoe broke the mold.

Although my mother loved him dearly, and ensured I grew up

respecting and loving him, he was not necessarily a holiday staple.

He attended all the big moments in my life from the lowered window

of a range of Cadillacs and limos.

I enjoyed a festive couple of hours aboard the Night Owl. Prior to

departing made sure to properly thank Champagne and Caviar for the evening's lesson in anatomy and movement, I think they call it by the more proper name of Yoga these days. Following the weaving footprints in the sand I made my way wearily towards home base. A hoarse but viable Squeak, Squeal, Squawk, told me I had safely reached my destination.

The glory of good aged whiskey, is the quality and the ages of experience I have drinking it. No hangover. I could smell breakfast piping hot and ready. No numbers to dial, no waiting for room service, and no being told that pajamas, Lauren or otherwise, are not appropriate dining room attire. The bar area, had been transformed to a cheerfully sunlit eating area, including beautiful white lilies on each table. I was starving. Kary was already up and at 'em, chomping on waffles, tearing little pieces and dipping them in strawberry syrup while reading what I can only guess was the society section.

"Good morning sunshine, your piece make it to page 6?" I inquired, curious to know if her late departure was worth my Bertha time spent.

"Mimosa?" Nyla greeted me with fresh drink in hand. I would soon come to know, and love, her uncanny knack for popping up, drink in hand, out of nowhere. And damn if she looked none the worse for the wear from the introductory night of meet, greet, and yacht creep. She wore a sheer cream cover-up over what could only be pieces of string masquerading as a polka dot bikini. Her hair hung in a long high ponytail that reached down to the finger path smooth tip of the arch of her back.

Kary kindly broke my stare. If looking straight through a person can do such things. "Yeah, it did. Today's the big day too. Ready?"

I toasted my glass questioningly, "Am I?" And gave her a side grin, trying tried to be nonchalant and cool but I think I was excited, well almost excited as she was. If the BYOY pre-party was any indication of things to come, this was going to be grand.

Breakfast was delicious; waffles, pancakes, biscuits, turkey sausage, some kind of veggie patty, not too bad, but not too much eaten. All accompanied by fresh fruit, nuts, orange marmalade and four kinds of syrup. We had dined on deck and enjoyed more Mimosas in the afternoon sun, mine with a whiskey chaser of course. Alone at one of the tables, Kary and I engaged in one of our favorite past times, people watching. It was hilarious watching the late rising party goers from last night, creep around the upper decks like the living dead and shirk sunlight like Barnabas Collins himself. We laughed at the floppy hats and flabby butts, saggy tits and too low slung sarongs; and at the equal parody of enhanced bodies that basted on deck. The new age vampire, that doesn't melt in the sun.

Lunch for me was of the liquid variety while Kary and Nyla went shopping for last minute touch up items for the opening night festivities.

I lounged on deck, Aviator Ray-Bans on, underneath an umbrella with some new designer's logo I didn't recognize. Yes, I do know designers. Kary wouldn't have it any other way. The girl's birthday lasts a whole month. Peter and Nyla, being the spectacular socialites they were, often received "gifts" from upcoming designers hoping for a shot at the big shots. According to Kary: on Nyla, on runway, on street. Yes, in that order. Nyla, the fashion Santa.

I felt my glass cool in my hand and the weight of air to liquid shifted favorably. I lifted my shades slightly, to see gleaming white teeth rivaling all the brightness of the sun. But as my eyes traveled up, the slight curl that fell casually across Peter's forehead did a poor job of disguising the menace in his eyes as he refilled his own glass as well.

Peter ever so gently broke the awkward silence. "So Abe, our dear Kary seems quite taken with you. What's up?" I think he kind of glared. But, I'm funky enough to kind of let it slide, kind of. The thing about breaking that type of silence with this type of question, is the silence goes but the awkward hangs out. Ice cold. Peter was nothing if not blunt and to the point.

But seriously, where was this going? Er, be cool. "That's just Kary. We go back a ways."

Peter, solemn face and definite glare, "We go back a lifetime."

Point taken, but again, where was this going?

"Kary's our girl. She loves and she loves hard. Not often, and not as carefree as she would have it seem. Be careful with her Abe. We got her covered: here, now, forever, and all points in between…you dig."

He followed that statement with a stare at me in that 'eat shit and die' kind of way. As much as I hated to, I broke away from his gaze. Not the time, place, or person. But never one to abate, I responded coolly, "Peter, with all due respect. Kary and I are just friends. Good, close friends. I don't have any one else like her in my life and probably never will. Kary doesn't care if I have money or where I come from. She sees my talent, my person. She sees me."

"Humph", he smirked. Peter looked me dead in the eye. "And you here as her friend, as her close friend, I do care."

I noticed for the first time since I met him, both his eyes and glass were empty. We shared a silence of wills that transitioned into a discussion of the slow jazz tunes playing on the AM station from the yacht bridge.

A foreboding shadow loomed, blocking out the early afternoon sun. I lifted my shades to see a large speedboat pulling up dangerously close as it slowed alongside Peter's yacht.

I sat up in the lounger as I watched a thinly built gentleman climb aboard. I hung back a little as Peter rose to greet him. They spoke briefly out of range, and then Peter turned and motioned me over to the group. "Abe, meet Joely. He's a good friend of mine from childhood and will be joining our little group during the stay; a good man of whom to know." There was that smirking smile again, as his eyes met mine. Joely did not appear to note the exchange.

Joely: slim build, verging on very lean. He wore white slacks, a white cotton Ralph Lauren button-up – with a navy blue scarf, for effect I guess, and classic boat shoes. He looked as sly as a fox, and just as lean and hungry. A good man, of whom to know.

Peter invited Joely aboard for quick cocktails before we each went our separate ways to prepare for the grand opening festivities. As we said our goodbyes, the girls were pulling up in a small boat, loaded with packages. Kary and Nyla greeted Joely with passing smiles and air kisses, exchanging glances as they passed him. I would ask Kary about him should we get the chance to be alone this evening.

I dressed quickly, in a simple Calvin Klein cream linen suit and huarache sandals. The girls prepped and giggled while I guzzled. Peter, surprisingly as I had a silent bet with myself as to who would take longer – him or the girls, joined me a short time later. He wore a tailored dark cream dashiki, matching pants with fitted ankles, and cloth shoes with rubber soles. Dashing, damn it.

We engaged in idle gossip, which was liberating, as Peter did not initially seem the type. I hoped this was a sign that he was becoming more comfortable with me. I had to admit to myself, I wanted to belong. I spent so many years being Abe the writer, the thinker, the observer. Not that those are not genuine aspects of my character. But it can be, at times, more out of defiance to the decadence that surrounds me. I'm no saint, of course. I could choose to hang out with a crowd of less fortune. But honestly, with my looks and impeccable sense of style, the Abe of the 70's is just too funky for that.

"Here, I'll trade you." Nyla handed me a fresh glass of whiskey. Uncanny. I did not even hear her come into the room.

Nyla was devastatingly beautiful. She wore a cream-colored body hugging dress with an Empire waist trimmed with gold rope and balloon sleeves embroidered in gold lace. Her dark hair was pulled back into a high wide ponytail with a gold rope beaded headband. She wore matching pearl and gold bead dangling hoops. Peter took her around her slender waist and they waltzed to the light jazz sounds coming from the record player. Enchanted, my spell broken only by the light evening musk and jasmine perfume scent that slowly filled the room; I turned into my own vision of beauty, Kary Parsons. She was stunning. Her light cream dress hit all the right places. My eyes got lost in the journey from her diamond adorned neck to the soft skin beckoning between the deeply cut V that stopped just above her navel. Not wanting to spoil the moment, I mouthed, "You look wonderful." She grinned and reached for my arm, as her escort to Cornerstone. A Million dollars.

We reached the landing where the Cornerstone transportation ferry was waiting to take guests to the main island, on which the resort was built. The ferries were extravagant events in and of themselves. An open bar, member cards and confetti packets were waiting for each guest. Each card personalized, the Cornerstone Black card – a onetime issue to tonight's guests that ensured all the privileges that wealth required during future Cornerstone Resort visits.

When we boarded for our turn to be whisked away to Cornerstone, we were directed to the on-board membership deck.

Kary, Peter, and Nyla, went forward to receive their packets.

Kary leaned over and whispered to me: "You're my guest Abe, so you can use my card. You are under my reservation so there shouldn't be any issues. We're a team". She smiled.

Peter glanced over and interrupted our mental arm in arm skip down the lane. "Actually Kary (so much for the subtle whisper), that won't be necessary. Abe." He gestured toward me (I am not going to be this guy's guppy all month). I looked at the package in his hand. There was my name, bold as day.

Kary smiled and squeezed my arm "Oh how cool, you got one too. This place is so exclusive! I mean they even cater to your guests on an occasion like this." By "guests" I take it to mean those not quite fortuned enough to warrant an exclusive invite. Kary speak translation.

Peter's eyes met mine, with a smirk to end all smirks, "Indeed, how COOL indeed."

His gaze was locked and definitely loaded. I wanted to believe my return gaze clearly stated: stand down, man. But when breeze met brow, the gentle moisture told me otherwise. For once, I opted out of the trip to the bar, choosing instead to enjoy the cool lake air on the upper level deck. The ferry gently whisked us towards Cornerstone Resort, shrouded in cream.

The transport ferries stood in a line, a few yards from the island. All passengers were asked to gather on one of the three deck levels, while we approached. As we drew nearer, the air filled with calypso music. It started with a low jingle and escalated into a full-on cacophony of sound, surrounding us on every side. In the process the shroud slowly rose to reveal the most magnificent and magical sight my well-travelled eyes had ever fell upon. The lights in all of Michigan must have flickered when they flipped the switch to turn on Cornerstone. The luminescence and grandeur was the eigth wonder of the world, for real.

Squeal, Squeak, Squawk! We had arrived!

Passengers were unloaded in an orderly fashion and directed to the large outdoor stage arena. If this were Sodom and Gomorrah, they would all be pillars of salt, as they strained their necks to look back at the resort area.

Excitement reached a fever pitch as we followed the cobblestone road to the stage. Kary had a media pass so we were all front and center, careful not to miss a thing. A hushed silence fell over the crowd as the stage curtain went up with the sound of a chorus and music that could only be described as evangelical.

The proceedings that took place over the next forty-five minutes were five stars by anybody's measure. The Band played a nice mix of jazz and funk that got the crowd swaying and focused on the stage. Fireworks shot up from the corners in the Cornerstone colors of cream, red, gold and green. A chorus line of girls kicked their way across the large stage. Drum roll and a booming voice over the loudspeaker announced, the one and only Billy "The Showman Collins" Shakely – per Peter and my idle gossip – Billy, aka, B.C. to his friends and B.S. to a less than fortunate few.

The Showman did not disappoint. Taking center stage, Billy was dressed in a red suit, cream tie, gold rope chain with a pearl and diamond and emerald encrusted medallion that, upon close observation, spun like a wheel of chance. Murmurs of excitement waved over the crowd as Billy delivered his welcome speech.

Ladies and Gentlemen: Welcome to a place like no other on earth. [Wavering Chorus] Cornerstone Resort, delivers only the finest, shiniest, blinding-est good time and fellowship that you will ever find, want or need. [Organ]. Be prepared to be razzled, dazzled, and for the faint of heart, frazzled [B.C. shimmy dip] at the magnificence designed with only the wealthy in mind. At Cornerstone Resort we have thought of your every desire. Our diamond star Casino, invites you to spend what you can spare, and a little more if you dare. Our luxury villas offer you a home away from home, and it ain't nobody's business if you don't sleep here alone. Our world class chefs provide culinary delights, so indulge in the temptation and satisfy your every appetite. Our disco on the water entices you to boogie away the night. Our deluxe spa will keep your weave tight, your wig right and your body feeling dynamite! Fellas can relax in our state of the art media center and cigar rooms, and the world famous Midas Lounge, where Champaign ain't just a city in Illinois. Folks, check out our 24-hour concierge and activity center located in the main building where our friendly and professional staff can attend to you and ensure you wish and want for nothing at your Cornerstone Residence. Let no desire pass, cause with B.C. around, all a Playa' got to do is ask!

[Music; dun, dun, dun, dun]

And the band played on…~

We were organized into groups of Red, Gold, Green, or Cream and escorted to our villas. Once inside we could arrange to join the tour groups that would be running throughout the week. Kary immediately signed up. I, however, chose to explore on my own; certain she would fill me in on anything I overlooked.

The Cornerstone Resort Villas, were truly amazing and definitely not my home away from home. They made my two-room suite, luxury accommodations look like a holding cell. First of all the Villas area could more easily be described as a small village.

Each villa had two scooters parked in a small carport. Residents could also ring for a chauffeur limo inspired golf cart, if such transportation were so desired. The villas were a short comfortable walk from the Welcome Center and Entertainment Complex. There was a small playground and children's activity center, which for the most part, none of us would be exploring. Children conveniently placed out of sight: nannied up, and presumably out of mind.

I gave myself a quick tour of our three-bedroom, four-bathroom villa. There was a full dining area, small kitchen, and complimentary maid service, full butler service for the larger villas at the far end of the village; and most importantly, a fully stocked bar. The living space was tastefully, but opulently, decorated. If it is possible for the two to exist in harmony. A separate office area occupied a side room. The bedrooms were spacious, each with a walk in closet, dressing area, bathroom en-suite, and a small balcony overlooking the meticulously manicured grounds complete with a spectacular view of Lake Michigan. Lush greenery surrounded each private villa outdoor patio area. Just beyond the sliding doors were a patio, fire pit, small pool, and lounge area.

It was getting late into the evening, and I begin to realize my exhaustion. Kary had decided to join the press tour that hit the highlights. She wanted to send an early morning, firsthand account over the wire to all the major society columns.

Hungry, I decided now was as good of a time as any to test out the culinary delights and delivery service. Cornerstone, considered a residence, did not use the term room service. I ordered a turkey avocado and sprout sub with homemade kettle chips from the gourmet deli. I bypassed my usual whiskey for the bottle of Dom chilling in our room; anxiously anticipating our timely arrival. I settled out on the patio and consumed the deliciously prepared gourmet toasted sandwich and chips. I took a page from Marilyn's book and enjoyed the remaining chips with the last of the Champagne. Palette pleased, it was time for a whiskey and rest. Alas, the best laid plans.

The villa phone rang loudly, disrupting my retreat from the mayhem. Peter, cool, calm, collected on the other end, "Abe, the guys and I are heading out for a nightcap and to check out the cigar room. We'll be by in ten."

"Solid." I replied, exhausted and fully aware it was useless to argue.

Peter arrived in one of the mini golf carts, surprisingly, sans chauffeur, none of that scooter shit for the far-enders. Joely, looking as slick as oil, accompanied Peter.

The cigar lounge was appropriately dimmed and amazingly well-ventilated. Peter led us to group of men settling in around a plush seating area, and drink orders promptly delivered. Mr. Abe, your whiskey neat. I likes the cigar lounge.

Peter entered the seating area and majestically introduced me to his court. "Greetings and Salutations friends. Abe, meet the friends." Peter introduced me to Mortimer, the resident playboy. "Mortimer is quite the visionary; the only one of our group to be smart enough to stay single preceding the advent of hot pants. Been following his stock tips religiously ever since." I nodded my drink in homage to his wisdom.

Mortimer wore one of the slim fitting polos of the day, in a designer red. Red and green plaid pants, slim-fitting as well; opting for a slightly lower platform shoe in lizard skin green. Mortimer offered a firm handshake and dimpled smile that would melt butter.

Peter then directed my attention to the other side of the sitting area. "And here, just beyond the cloud of smoke is Topher."

Topher leaned forward, emerging from the cloud, of thick cigar smoke. "How ya' doin'". Topher: built larger than the rest of the men in the group – more bulky, in the non-athletic sort of way; but judging from his handshake, in shape enough. Call it instinct, but for whatever reason, I instantly did not like this guy. Maybe because he was oozing a veneer that demanded I should.

Introductions completed. I settled into a seat observing the group as I awaited my refill.

I always considered myself attractive; classic good looks, handsome is not a stretch. But, the men of Cornerstone, as I termed them, were movie star good looking. Newman, Redford, Brando, Cooper, Grant, me-not-in-their-league-handsome and debonair.

Here is another one as I speak. A figure slightly masked by the dim lighting, sitting across from me, a smooth cat. Legs crossed, Fedora low, leaned back, one arm extended, resting lazily on the back of the couch; skillfully blowing circles of smoke between long, slow drags on the cigar. I'm briefly mesmerized by the round wisps rising, one after the other; methodically precise in the dimly lit pit, and dissipating into thin air. Through the clearing smoke, the deepest pair of brown eyes I'd ever seen looked up at me. In this light they appeared jet black. A tongue darted to the corner of full, plush lips, lightly moistened and glistening like diamonds in gin, surely sinful. I shifted uncomfortably with the stare, with my own thoughts. This is the gentleman's cigar lounge after all. I've never reason to question my sexual preference, so the current stirring was quite unwelcome. I was in need of some serious clarification. They don't want no repercussions up in here. As Uncle Roscoe would say: No jiving. I caught a soft chuckle from Peter as he leaned forward and extended his hand in the strangers' direction. I guess my change in disposition was duly noted.

Peter gently tapped my arm, "Abe, I have been remiss in my introductions. Our final group member this evening," he tilted his head "pardon the oversight," he smirked at the gentleperson seated across from us. "Abe, meet Jai, *She* (he stressed) prides herself on her dominion over illusion and androgyny. Let that not deter or unravel you my friend. She is loyal, trustworthy and downright dogged in her pursuits."

I believe their matching sneers canceled each other out and landed me right in the middle of a D.C. comic. I half wanted to glance around for the trusty sidekick; but the waiter with a fresh drink worked out fine in a crunch.

Leaning forward, the undone buttons on her cream collared men's shirt revealed two handful-sized clues that I clearly missed in the dark shadows earlier. Jai initiated a firm but warm handshake. She wore dark green trousers, a cream shirt, and gold and red pinstriped semi-tailored vest, dark men's trouser socks, and dark green and cream Stacy Adams. The low-sitting dark green fedora hid her long, feminine lashes and the aforementioned full lips in the dim light.

Jai extended her hand to shake. "Jai – Julia Anna – but you mustn't. Somebody has to dude up these divas. One more loose lock flopping gently over the forehead and this makeshift saloon will have one O too many." She leaned her head back and delivered a deep throaty laugh. I lifted my drink as a mask over which to continue to gaze and joined in her laughter; mesmerized, relieved, intrigued.

Catching my gazing, Topher, winked and smiled, "Brooks Brothers never looked so good, huh? Can't crease out all the curves! Ha, Ha brotha." Witty, but enough. I so did not like this guy.

We finished off our nightcaps, with talk of the shroud lifting, suspecting loaned crop planes, helicopters, balloons, what have you, and the extravagance of the whole extravaganza. Peter rounded up the group to transport us back to our villas. Jai declined the offer, opting to enjoy the cool night air with a leisurely walk home. I, being a gentleman, offered to walk her home.

What is with these people and the "eat shit and die" look. I playfully responded "Careful sista, those claws do retract don't they." That got a laugh. I then cleverly surmised, headed as we both were to the same area, we might as well share the sidewalk in that direction. Nodding in acknowledgement of the cold stare, I walked a casual distance next to her arms-folded self towards the villas. Fedora and all, the moonlight caught the soft smile on her lips.

Still a short distance to go. Arm stretch, re-fold. Jai opened the door for conversation, which was cool, cause I'm not so funky I can't admit a wee bit of admirable intimidation. She prodded gently, "So New York? What do you think of Michigan so far?"

"Not what I thought, but then again Cornerstone is not exactly a classic introduction to Midwestern life. As a writer I like the diversity, a quiet cabin in the UP (Upper Peninsula) woods, for a serene setting, the Manufacturing town backdrop of Detroit for the inner city struggle, and a gun racked pickup truck with a deer strapped to the hood for all points between in a plot crunch. Good Stuff."

She actually laughed. She recovered and reflected, "Then there's us rich fuckers, who buy and design any experience, ambience or temporary setting to suit. We make, we break. That little piece that builds our core, our cornerstone, our foundation. We hold onto it for life. We have others believing in it for us, even at the cost of life. The pyramids, the plantations, hell even the Arch, people gave lives to keep us grand."

I nodded silently in agreement and duly noted my confirmed admiration. She seemed a little different than the others. That was a not too bad a thing. Our shared portion of the pavement ended. I wanted to kiss her cheek good night. Although bright, the moon would not offer enough light for me to find all the pieces of my face if I did. She tilted her hat and headed down the cobblestone path to her villa. I half bowed. Well, how the hell else do you bid goodnight to one with dominion over illusion and androgyny? Then I headed down my own cobblestone path.

I reached my villa. Exhausted, I braced myself, but the only squeak I heard was my slick soles on the freshly polished marble floor. ~

Kary did not ask when I got in, and I did not ask when she got in. We're not like that.

I woke up to the smell of fresh hot coffee and came down to an array of pastries and whole fruits. I could hear Kary pecking away on the typewriter in the side room office area. I did wonder how long she'd been working. Still shirtless, in my soft cotton lounging pants, I poured two cups of coffee, both black and strong, one no sugar, and the other one teaspoon of bourbon, as measured by the quarter cup. Libations in hand I headed to the office area.

"Break?" I held up the coffee cup. I smiled down at Kary, seated in the latest Herman Miller office chair and hunched over the typewriter, her hair up in a hastily wrangled ponytail. She looked fresh and awake.

Her gaze, following the cup as extended, managed to land on my chest. I was confident in my muscular frame, smooth chest, and strong biceps. Kary's lingering eye told me I was a little too comfortable, but rightly confident. I chuckled to myself. I was so used to being alone in my hotel room it didn't occur to me to cover up, so to speak. Kary shyly turned her attention to the steaming cup. The warmth in the room did little to beckon my robe. I backed out of the room, with a slight off balance trip, somewhat gracefully and grabbed a t-shirt from my gym bag in the corner of the living room.

Tension eased as Kary standing in the office doorway, giggled. "Nice shirt."

So it was a little fitted. It was after all, meant to be worn at that human fruit stand commonly referred to as the Gym.

"Nice robe," I childishly retorted. Her robe had shifted, revealing a very soft looking silk nightie with a very low scoop neck, in a very pretty, perky soft pink.

She grinned, "Touché", and made a loose attempt at tying the robe.

I crossed the room and opened the sliding door. "Ah, a breeze."

Kary joined me on the patio and we watched the late morning sun rise higher in the sky. Kary asked "Would you like to join the others for brunch around one?"

"Sounds Good". I began to tell her about my evening at the cigar lounge, and she filled me in on a few details.

Peter, an investment tycoon, was into mergers and takeovers. He put companies on the social and commercial map. Peter was the guy who knew the secretaries' kids birthdays and their six-month or twentieth-year anniversaries. Peter, therefore, knew when great men were at their most vulnerable. He was essentially in the making and breaking business. Peter by all accounts had clean hands. Joely on the other hand, no pun intended, was the dirt under his nails. Joely was the guy who knew guys. Apparently, he was the son of the estate manager at Peter's family home. Growing up around the very well to do, Joely learned to do well.

Mortimer was a single technologies magnate. He was born in Japan and adopted by a wealthy American couple. He was a MIT graduate with a computer engineering and science degree. He was currently working with a team to make the computer a personal experience. Mortimer's company motto was striving towards digital excellence means a computer in every household. Accessibility over affordability being what it was, the 'every' had its qualifiers.

Mortimer met Jai while at MIT. They dated for a couple of years, but drifted apart to friends, as far as Kary knew. Jai found she was more interested in the motherland than motherboards. Finding her way into sculpting, photography, and painting, she spent a semester abroad touring Africa and Asia for a little ancestral inspiration. Jai's mother is black and her father Asian. Jai did quite well with her "Ethnic Designs." She wanted to go bi-coastal and start an interior design company, but needed sound investors. Her family, Kary supposed, had higher aspirations. They were more than happy to fund her heiress lifestyle. They even considered it a small investment in her future with hopes of her finding an appropriate suitor. Julia Anna's parents were eager to resume building their dynasty, rather than that of Bloomingdales and supplementing the Harry Winston fortune. I wondered how that Julia Anna transferred to the present day Jai. Jai's friends were her biggest supporters and considered her artwork worthy investments and future heirlooms. In terms of actually financing her efforts, I guess the old saying goes, 'don't shit where you eat. Shop not stock, you dig.

Lastly, Topher. Topher, always somewhat of an outsider, gained admittance and therefore acceptance, or rather tolerance, among the group – and thus proper society – through his long, long term girlfriend Madeline. Madeline, whom I've yet to meet. Topher owned two elite retirement villages, one in Chicago, Illinois, and one in Detroit, Michigan.

He also founded a charitable foundation that was quite profitable. Their work was to provide comfortable hospice for wealthy patrons. The clients being the children or family members of the mentally infirmed seeking agency workers to provide twenty-four hour care, maintenance and monitoring of their loved ones. With all the social obligations and financial transactions to be governed, they had all the love, just none of the time to devote. Enter Topher, his rest/retirement villages, and the Foundation.

Kary was just getting to the good stuff: some suspected the charity and rest homes were more aligned to the needs of the beneficiaries of the infirmed. The charitable donations – cough, cough – were small investments in futures, ensuring a comfortable quiet end to a rich full life. "Father needn't suffer unnecessarily…" Drift gotten, as the villa phone rang inside. It was Nyla reminding us about brunch, we were half an hour late already.

That's the thing about Kary Parsons. She was easy to look at, easy to talk to, easy to listen to, easy company – like the song says, 'easy like Sunday morning'.

Kary told Nyla we were heading their way shortly, "Abe, time sure flies, huh? A cup of coffee goes a long way." She smiled. "We better change and hurry over. This group can get very inventive when left to their own imaginations regarding two people's alone time." Her eyes searched mine.

"I'm sure they can come up with something better than us getting it on in here, talk about overactive imagination." I chuckled over my shoulder as I bounded up the stairs.

During my quick shower, I thought about what I said and how. If Kary was hurt she didn't show it, but I didn't exactly meet her eyes when I said it either, the robe had slipped a little. I know she likes me, to be all middle school about it, but she can't really take that seriously, right? We both know what she knows of me, I'm just not enough. I drink, I write, I observe. She's just, she knows she can be too chatty, materialistic, bratty, excitable, expensive, annoying. Was the mirror smiling because I forgot obnoxious? "Easy like Sunday morning", I found myself singing aloud.

I got done before her, even though she had showered before she started working earlier. I nursed a small swallow of whiskey while I waited. I looked up as I heard her coming down the stairs. Oh she was hurt. Her outfit showed me so. Snaps! She wore an emerald green, TCB. (Taking Care of Business) yellow diamond collared, tight fitting, bell bottom, halter-style jumpsuit with strappy gold platform heels and her Farrah Hair. Her green eyes sparkled, my mouth dropped. No subtle way to connect my upper and lower lips, so I spread them into a wide grin.

"Nothing to the imagination here" I said. The nice thing about meaning what you say, and your heart knowing what you feel, is that it all meets up in the eyes. I was truly sorry for my flippancy about Kary's crush. Furthermore, I deserved for her to be in that 'and you're with him'… too-gorgeous-to-be outfit. The cost of that get up, she knew her investment paid dividends. I meet her at the stairs. I extended my hand. She took it and grinned. A million dollars, easy.

As we walked to the entertainment complex, we bantered about whether our conversation earlier was gossip or not: started by me thanking her for the juicy gossip. In the end, being writers, we both agreed it was more about character backstory. Insight into the key players, subject background, character development, it worked for us. Even though the afternoon was cool, my hand felt moist squeezed against hers.

We could see Nyla leaning over the Penthouse roof veranda railing. Nyla, waving and whoo-hooing! "KP" she shouted.

"On our way" KP returned. Yup, full lung capacity both ways.

We joined the group on the veranda, just off the dining room. Brunch was laid out; a variety of fresh baked breads, garlic cheese biscuits, banana nut bread, some multi-grain number my stomach lurched me past, and onto lox, grilled salmon, whitefish patties, turkey sausages, fruit platters, various cheeses, nuts, spreads and sauces. Included in this array were the breakfast requirements of champions, caviar, and mimosas. There were also some new fangled wine spritzers, but no whiskey. I sampled the liquid refreshments as I perused the buffet. I eventually settled on a few of the offerings and stocked my plate. Kary opted for the breakfast of champions. I joined the group seated in the lavish outdoor lounge area and fire pit. There was a nice breeze from the water, but not strong enough to warrant lighting the fire.

Peter, Nyla, Topher, Joely, Jai, Kary, and I engaged for the afternoon. As my plate was almost empty, I was able to tune in and enjoy the conversation around me. They were discussing one of their first group gatherings.

"Remember the Franklins?" Kary posed to the group.

"More like the Franklinsteins," Jai piped up.

"Oh, they were just eccentrics with very eclectic tastes." Peter chimed in.

"No dear," entered Nyla, "they were all out ghoulish."

Joely laughs, "Their dude creeped me out, Lurch Jr."

"They had the creepiest domestics I have ever encountered." Kary said.

"Remember how they would just pop up out of nowhere, 'are you being served?' " Jai said through a crooked smile, "I think it was more about servicing you for Lurch Junior, Kary."

They all howled. Kary turned to me. "I think that's where Nyla learned the uncanny drink service you so adore."

With that Nyla got up and slunk around the seats, stopping in a 'duck, duck, goose' fashion at one or the other of us. "Are you being served", she'd say in a gnarly English accent.

When she got to Peter, he pulled her over the couch headfirst and said, "Now I am!"

We all broke out in giggles and laughs. It was interesting to watch them play like children in a monopoly world: where the money was very real, the Parker Brothers were your actual neighbors, your best friend was the banker for real, and your family already owned a hotel on Boardwalk.

It was well after 3:00 PM, which meant I was for real behind in meeting my daily whiskey quota. My finger almost met nose when I raised my hand for the waiter assigned to our group, right as he was in the process of bending down to ask me if I needed service. I guess creepy domestics are universal on the high end service of things.

There was some light jazz coming through the outside speakers. The guys played name the tune and artist. The girls discussed Jai's new designs and inspirations from her most recent travels. I caught bits and pieces of each group, but heard all the whiskey draining from my glass. I got up to stretch my legs in the direction of the bar.

Looking towards the doorway, I wondered for the first time, if ever, if I had one too many already. The image before me made me wonder if Foster Grant started making beer goggles, or if the woman in front of me was really that beautiful. Either the room fell silent, or all the blood rushing to the sensory organs in my body made me deaf and motionless, I was admittedly stunned.

I momentarily felt Jai brush against me lightly and whisper, "That would be Madeline." Jai smiled slyly as she went to greet Madeline. She and Madeline walked passed me arm in arm. And I had a rare misstep at being the coolest cat in the room; it was somehow belied by my ear to ear grin. The air filled with light white musk and sandalwood, the veranda filled with Madeline. Her deep skin tone glistened like sunlight on the water. Her dark brown eyes shone, the whites like foam on waves, her hair like fresh seaweed on a dark sand beach. Her lips parted like the red sea, promising safe passage at her command to those worthy, lucky, faithful, blessed, and Topher.

Errr! What? Did that name just come from those deep Bordeaux painted lips? She breezed easily past me and straight into Topher's arms. This was Topher's Madeline. I really, really, don't like this guy. I watched her kiss him lightly. She puckered to flat unresponsive lips. He held his arms possessively around her waist. Grinning…sly fox bastard. I wanted to stomp my feet like a seven-year-old on the baseball diamond as my nemesis rounded to home plate. Not Fair! Instead, I did what any thirty-plus young man would do, I called for a whiskey double.

I could feel Jai's hard stare, and averted my eyes in accordance to the very bottom of my glass. She introduced me to Madeline from my perch across the seating area. Madeline and I exchanged waves. I caught Jai's eye and 'thank you' winked. She bounce tapped a finger to her fedora, a 'you're welcome' nod. She thoughtfully allowed distance between Topher, Madeline and me. I had originally thought she was being catty with the whisper and stare earlier, but she was just being Jai and observant, like Eden Abe. I should have known, it's hard to be catty in Brooks Brothers suspenders and trousers.

It was early evening and the sun had long been nestled in its rightful place high above the clouds. The conversation livened as they made plans for the evening. I smiled and nodded along; Kary would take care of us in all the planning.

I contemplated the surroundings. In this moment, I realized I was different here too. Or maybe because I cared for things I had long abandoned. As exemplified in the fact that assholes date beautiful women all the time in New York. I knew nothing about Madeline other than that she was beautiful. She could have a heart as black as her hair, but somehow I doubted it. Yes, I was different here, because I had become expectant versus observant. I had a taste of frivolous indulgence, and it should have been enough. Pack your bags. Thank Kary, and go home, Abe. However, I knew I would not. I knew what foundations built Cornerstone. I knew the set, the craving, how it thrived, what it promised. What I did not know was what it delivered. And for that, I knew even then what I know now, I want in.

~

As dusk fell upon the veranda, we respectively drained glasses, confirmed plans for dinner, and said momentary goodbyes. As we filed into the lobby and elevator, I watched Madeline covertly from behind. She was ample, pleasing enough, more bang than bounce. I smiled, I hoped only on the inside. I noticed how nicely the white slip dress hung loosely onto her frame. It complimented her beautifully. It was not lost on me that I noticed her dress as an afterthought. Is it so wrong, the first time you meet a woman, to view her as God intended? Nope. Is it wrong to breathe her in and sniff her like a dog in heat if her backside is crushed up against you in a crowded elevator: see above.

We had agreed to reconvene at 7:30 PM for a late dinner; resolute to have pre-dinner cocktails at 6:30 PM on the veranda, our spot. Since we only had a couple hours before meeting up again, Kary showered as soon as we returned to our villa. I showered the back of my throat with a whiskey, as cold as I could stand it. I felt fucking menopausal. Hot flash, Madeline. Kary came rushing down the stairs in a frantic search for some must have diamond of one sort or another. I would swear on a fully stocked liquor cabinet she had a shopping bag or clothes in every room; one big endless closet.

"What's up Loch Ness" I joked. She was soaking wet, face covered in a green gook and hair battling ferociously with her poppy decorated shower cap.

"Eat ass, Abe" she retorted.

"I wasn't aware it was on the menu, should I bring my own dipping sauce?" I bellowed heartily, and playfully slapped at lower towel as she ran past me. I caught her grinning as she soaked the stairs with sea salt infused exfoliating cream footprints.

"What's gotten into you?" she snickered. What indeed? I was well, jovial, and looking, as Kary would say, 'ever so' forward to the evening ahead. I chomped on whiskey flavored ice and headed up for my own frantic grooming session.

I took extra care in my appearance. I showered with the Aramis gift set my mom had given me for my birthday, rather than the pilfered hotel supplied toiletries in which I usually indulged. I dried off with a fluffy cream towel and began to build the masterpiece. Kary had

her Fashion Fair, I had my dumbbells. I hit the quick bicep pumps.
Flex. Push-ups, flex, sit-ups, flex, mirror check, Mr. Olympia pose,
and done. I apply a dab of dippity-do-dah to slick and shine the hair.
Opt to rock the facial stubble, so just a quick line up; and moisturize
the face. My mama taught me that. "Moisturizing is the fountain of
youth Abe", she would say. The smooth-skinned boyishly charming
face that stared out at me from the mirror, I thank mama for that. The
angular jaw line, stoic nose, high cheekbones, seductive dark eyes
and full lips, I thank mom and dad for. And the fact that I'm a
Scorpio, well I gotta thank daddy for his timing. Mirror to Abe:
'You's a bad mother…' Abe to Mirror, 'Shut yo' mouth.' And I
flashed it a set of perfectly aligned pearly whites.

I guess I took a considerably longer time than my usual 'shit,
shower, and shave', as Kary was already downstairs when I got to
the sitting area. I heard various sounds of funk blaring from the in
room stereo. I stepped straight into a whiskey on ice and a vision of
paradise. She wore a Versace original, long, gold shimmering gown.
Very low cut, with a thin string of diamonds that looped once around
her neck and trickled like raindrops down a sun dusted Spanish cliff,

to a low abyss. She gleamed as I can only imagine did the streets of heaven. Casting my eyes down, the slit's opening rose from the bottom of the gown to meet at a point that reminded me, the devil is surely in the details. Her auburn hair was sweep into an elegant low, side ponytail, fastened with diamond tinsel strings. Her subtle makeup expertly applied. Her lips an inviting glossy pink; I watched them, glistening and full as she slipped the crystal glass between them; sipped, licked, and swallowed.

She handed me my full glass, "You want?"

I took. Fuck the hot flash, this was a full on heat wave. She giggled. I did some kind of crazy, undignified snort, which only made her giggle more. I shook my head and joined in the laughter. We cover awkward pretty well. I freshened my whiskey and refilled her martini from the decanter on the counter. Kary turned up the radio and started practicing the Hustle. She wanted to be good at it. God bless the earnest effort.

Kary spoke over the music, "Boy, if Eden club could see you now, all 'pretty boy'd up'".

I grinned, spread my hands, "I'm just lettin' it do what it do baby," and ended with a little dip.

Kary squinted her eyes with a smile and turned up the radio and Carly Simon, to sing along with *You're So Vain*. She glared in perfect pitch.

I countered with a pot et kettle kind of grimace.

We both erupted into laughter. I linked her arm in mine. "Let's roll, man". With that, we shut it down and danced into the cool night air.

Kary, now a few steps ahead, boogied down the lane, a different Carly Simon song, with James Taylor; a particular line from Mockingbird; popped in mind with no foreboding intentions. It was an ominous thought indeed cause we're not like that.

"…he's gonna surely break this heart of mine…"

When we arrived, Kary went in search of Nyla, and I went in search of Jameson. Empty veranda, no big; empty whiskey glass, a major issue. I didn't have to wait long. Cornerstone staff is top notch. Giles the, well "our" concierge on the/"our" veranda was ready with a fresh one. Thanks to our lofty home-base host I've no doubt. I was settled in one of the lounge sectionals, taking in the night air and waiting for Kary.

"Er-hum," seriously can he even play poker with that tell? I turned to Joely, standing at the far corner of the wrap around outdoor counter bar. The cream linen pant suit on his thin frames obscured him amongst the billowing cream curtains on their thin rods, covering a portion of the balcony fencing behind the bar.

"Uh, Hi" an octave louder then intended, covering awkward not so well.

I really did not know what to make of him. He didn't have that moneyed air, yet his background is betrayed only by his fierce loyalty to Peter, displayed at levels generally only demonstrated between oneself and one's Lord or counsel. His attention to Peter was a combination of subtle idolization, distilled envy, and determined equality. I thought 'what a strange limbo or purgatorious existence in a circle such as is the world of Peter and Nyla'. Guys to Gentlemen, sure they have enough to get in, but lack the breeding to "**be** in". 'Is there a point of break, a point of breech, when for the Lords coin the counsel doth reach?' I smile, and nod. Joely raises his glass in response.

White Musk and Sandalwood; stomach churn, turn, flip in disgust; Madeline and Topher, respectively. Topher pointed in my direction, I rose to greet them. Topher grinned and slapped my hand with a shake. Madeline smiled and waved. I really concentrated on not staring, wishing to God for some anti-eye popping device, or at least something that could dial it down a degree or ten. Lacking such resources in the present day, I gawked as Madeline lowered herself into one of the plush seats of the dark green sectional. She wore a Halston halter dress with alternating light and dark green panels. The skirt fell just above her knee in the front with a long flowing, floor-length train in the back. She crossed her legs as she sank back into to the deep soft pillows, revealing their well-toned length as light reflecting from the fire pit danced along the curve, playing into the smooth arch that delineated muscle and flesh. The gold straps of her wooden platform sandals wrapped around her calves all the way up to her knees, like mischievous fingers beckoning one to grasp, hold, and sinuously slide firmly towards the abyss, deeper, warmer, hotter than…

"Er, Oh Shit. Uh, excuse me." Not cool, slammed right into the fire pit. "They really need to find a better place for that."

"Someplace less awkward," Jai startled me from behind with her deep throaty sarcastic tone.

Madeline nervously rocked her crossed leg in a slow rhythm like the beating of a primal drum as she waited for Topher to return with their drinks.

I told myself whatever you do don't start talking about the weather. So naturally, "It's a nice breeze out here tonight".

Madeline smiled. Her soft, smooth, glistening Chanel Bordeaux lips spreading into a side smile: "And the writer speaks bravely of the weather. What no soliloquy on the earth, wind, and fire?"

"Not unless it is with writer and producer credit on the next album." I retorted, embarrassed but recovered, well-played Abe.

She laughed a deep hearty one from that toned, flat, sweet belly.

Jai snorted. My mind breathed "Bitch" into the wind.

I remixed my commentary on the weather and overall conversation starting "Madeline dearest, of the two works of heaven that surround me at present, I thought the topic of weather the fairest, because to speak on the topic of beauty in your presence, a chance the fair weather has'enth."

She folded her lips, licked, and gave a moistened 'Touché', "Better".

"Better; Better than suffer the wrath of Topher, don't want to disrespect."

"The wrath of Topher," she echoed. "Sounds like a cult classic." She laughed deeply again, subsiding into a soft giggle as we heard the clinking of ice signaling the aforementioned Topher's approach. Madeline sunk slowly back with her cool drink and gently tucked a stray curl behind her ear. I loosened the grip on my drinking glass, realizing I had been clenching it tightly in restraint. I'd wanted to caress the curl back into place the moment it broke free in her fits of laughter and joy. Topher joined us and lazily put his arm around Madeline. I went for a refill.

Kary, Peter and Nyla came laughing around the corner. Peter in cream linen pants, dark green alligator skin belt and matching shoes, a white cotton wide collar shirt with the top few buttons undone, and a gold Figaro link twenty-inch chain and matching bracelet. His gold and diamond studded wedding band glistened in the evening lights. Nyla sauntered in a few paces behind, and sparkling like pirate treasure; her dark blonde hair pulled back into a long braid that reached halfway down her back into a medley of brown and blond and golden and ruby tinsel. She wore a light green spaghetti-strapped, floor-length dress that clung tightly to her slender frame and fell at asymmetrical lengths. The low scooped back exposed gently tanned skin and copper glitter.

As we all settled into our seats, the entry way filled once again with laughter as Jai re-entered with Mortimer, obliviously in mid-debate. Mortimer insisting that one day Jai would be able to create competitively equal artwork by computer alone, Jai arguing the merits of the artistic process. "Honestly Mortimer" Jai quipped, rolling her head and eyes like she was auditioning for *The Exorcist*.

"Oh God, please stop them now." Kary jumped up playfully between them. "Before they sidebar into ethics, integrity, the bastardly spawn of art and electronics and other convoluted bullshit." She punctuated this by luring Mortimer into the rhythm of the funk radio station and doing the bump to the sounds of *Pop That Thang*, by the Isley Brothers, wafting from the speakers courtesy of the Showman Collins evening Funk Love radio hour. "Funk Love, Funk Love, and then Funk Your Mind".... If that shit Fuck's my mind, I'm suing. My mind was luckily, and oh so graciously, releasing to the intoxicating bump that had spontaneously erupted moments ago. I did not know you could bump so low. I chuckled to myself watching her slow easy moments, as if she were in a room all to herself, with no one watching at all…. Oh, but I am. Kary Parsons, a million dollars. Easy Money; Jameson agreed.

Giles entered the veranda and announced our table, so we dutifully filed out. Since I see the proverbial and literal glass as half full, I lingered to my last swallow. Peter, Nyla, Kary and Mortimer bounced blissfully along to the restaurant. Topher waved Joely in his direction and pushed Madeline towards mine.

"Ah, you mind" he gestured toward her waiting arm.

"Not at all" I smirked it.

"I thought not." Smirk remix, damn it.

He winked, turning to Joely, as Madeline linked her arm into mine. Her bare arms warm against my thin cotton shirt. I smiled down at her, as Topher leaned in the talk to Joely. 'Why the fuck do you need to whisper when you are the only two out here' I thought, until I caught the light whiff of cigar smoke.

"Yes, heaven forbid integrity and morals interfere with commerce and profit", the throaty sound played melodically through the sweet Havana mist. Jai assigned the post to stand on its own, gazed the scene dismally and crushed out her cigar in the freestanding ivory ashtray. I smiled, hesitantly extended my arm. Jai tipped and nod with the fedora and joined our chain. We bounced blitzedly along to the restaurant.

The dining room where we were seated was an extravaganza in and of itself. VIP, I guess, dining area was nestled over the water. The dark night glistened with running lights, subtle and somewhat muffled sounds of party goers; part of the mystique is the wonderment and mystery that belies how the other half, well more like three-fourths lives, but I digress. I looked out of the partially glassed-encased dining area onto the water and watched playfully-dancing lights chasing after each other. Hide and seek as they intersected the rippled flow of the cool lake; a man-made masterpiece to rival creation, or something like that. The big ceiling over the diners with its grand chandeliers in alternating ruby, emerald, and diamond baubles probably looked to the boat men and handlers on the outside like a carport on steroids. Thank God, Showman Shakely knew better than to class up the joint with alternating colored bulbs. Christmas in May, No spank you!

The meal in the main restaurant was served in courses. As Kary had stated there were alternative eating style joints throughout the property: buffet, grab n' go, traditional dining, and À la carte options. But this crew was five stars all the way. Dinner was an elegant, drunken, satiating feast. We laughed. We talked, debated, bantered and boasted, all within the boundaries of our raising; the restraints of proper decorum and all…then something about the Disco aka Funk Land.

Peter and Nyla excused themselves for a little after dinner ballroom dancing before meeting back up with us at, deep breath, Funk Land. The rest of us headed over to 'show'em how we do it now'. There was some kind of temporary malfunction with "BC's Ball of Love", so we detoured to the veranda to wait it out until Funk Land re-funktified itself.

We headed up to the veranda and Kary stopped at the host stand to get the names of the chefs for the VIP newsletter plus bragging rights to some of the fine dining elitists back in NYC.

As the rest of us rounded the corner, we heard the bane of all drunken existence, children's laughter…on "our" veranda. To see the queen of cool actually hyperventilate was one for the books alone. We would all crack up at Jai, after; but in the immediate we took the only logical approach there was, we sent in Jai and Madeline. Jai, she has that 'proud owner of a candy house in the woods' look. And Madeline, well, 'cause she's Madeline. Mortimer grinned; Casey Kasem ain't got nothin' on this countdown, 5-4-3-2-1….

Shrieks silenced. Veranda mass exodus. Mothers clutching children exeunt stage left, nannies stage right. Head-popped husbands, purses, and wives straight ahead. And that ladies and gents is called clearing the deck. We burst into giggles on the cleared battlefield. Needing to toast the vanquished, as we sank into the soft plush seating area, we motioned to Giles. Joely threw an abandoned binky over the balcony.

"That's cold-blooded" Topher chimed. We erupted with laughter and indulged in drank.

Nyla and Peter joined us, "Figured you guys were up here judging from the stampede in the hallway."

We regaled them tells of our feat. Secure our territory was amply marked, the ladies and Mortimer made haste to Funk Land.

I waved them on while I finished my drink. Being used to a somewhat, sometimes self-imposed, solitary moment back home, I needed a breather. I topped off my glass and moved to a quiet corner to breathe and enjoy the view. As I settled on post, I noticed Joely motion for Peter to hang back for a brief moment. Peter adjusted his collar and obliged. Or rather, granted Joely's wish. Peter and Joely begin speaking in whispered breaths.

In the open space, the voices carried. Joely was describing some sort of wealth-building seminar idea. Peter notably appeared to be listening with intent to Joely, who traditionally, well to my brief knowledge of him, was not generally so outspoken. Nor so animated; arms flaying, fist pumping...hopped up. Admittedly, a little awkward for the casual onlooker. I said casual, not curious. But even I know enough to shake the ice in my glass as an obligatory note of presence, just in case. And on cue, Peter, not one to be caught unaware, tapped Joely gently on the arm and turned the conversation down a degree or ten. Peter even attempted humor.

Interrupting Joely mid-sentence, Peter reached for Joely's glass. "Excellent observations Joely. In fact my friend, I think we're going to need a patent for that." He chuckled at himself.

In the sliver of moonlight covering the veranda, I could see the beads of perspiration forming on Joely's upper lip and forehead. For a man cooler than the shade, it was kind of a big deal.

Peter moved from behind the bar and a little closer to the opposite side of the veranda. I noticeably contemplated the sway of the tall trees in the distance, watching as they tap danced around the obvious.

Joely, cleared his throat and attempted to gain further validation whether for his idea, or person…well. He sipped slowly from the fresh glass, and spoke as he watched Peter for expression.

"So you think I could set something up? Maybe, incorporate. You know, I think it's a lotta cats out here, you know brothers, that could benefit. Spread the word about how to get our own. How to build wealth, investments, guidance, real shit, real money. You know."

"Indeed I do my friend. You know you are something of a protégé. Guidance is truly markedly profitable." Peter clasped his hands and rested his chin on his thumbs. Gazed off for a moment. His next words were spoken slowly, unequivocally and smooth as a rattlers belly, "A simple formula, a patent, a trademark, a small investment. Yes, in fact, I can set something up. You know; real shit, real money." He smiled raised his glass to Joely in a toast, patting him on the shoulder. "Thank you my friend. Thank you." The ice as the glass hit the cool granite…sheew, sheew, in quick succession.

Two of us winched as the knife pierced and turned. One of us strolled off the veranda with the moonlight at this back; and the last of the four men on the veranda stepped ominously from the shadows.

We all caught up with the ladies coming out to the powder room, and Mortimer looking glad to see us. And all together now, we head to get Funk'ed Up.

If there was a strobe light, globe light, disco ball or smoke machine left in Michigan it was still on the factory line, cause up in here, the Showman did the damn thing. We had to dance through a soul train just to get to the first bar, surprising us all by leading the pack…Jai. She clutched the fedora rim and pimp walked her way through the line.

"Go Jai, Go Jai". I told ya'll quintessential cool.

I let 'em know I got the moves and passed it off to Mortimer who took robotics to the stratosphere, tossing it to Peter and Nyla who put the O in tango, with an era defining Soulango. Oh yeah, that's gonna take. Madeline cat walked it. We called it Stomping Tongues, cause cats definitely had 'em out wagging. Now I don't mind a good sweat from time to time, but it increases the need for rehydration to an alarming level. So I made my way to the bar, let six shots of Cuervo run a train on me, and punished their bad behavior with two whiskey sours. Now, I'm ready for a drink.

Perfect timing, Peter secured us a cozy corner in VIP. If I take the stairs two at I time I should arrive in time for the first round.

"I saw you sweating it out down there. I didn't think you let that much alcohol leave your system at one time." Kary jabbed and giggled.

"I didn't see you at all", I retorted. Didn't want to have to wring out your do?"

"Ass" Kary grinned, a cool million. Mortimer saved her from future abuse by leading her to the dance floor. When it came to dancing well, Kary's got no soulango. We couldn't bear to watch. Time for round two.

I stood at the VIP balcony taking in all that was Funk Land and watching Kary re-construct all that I knew as dance. I glanced over to see Jai and Madeline engaged in deep conversation. Jai probably engaging in the, I hate Topher B-side. Madeline looking defeated, Jai looking, well, like a winner. Jai was lovely in the light of the flame. Dark eyes, hair shining, head in rhythmic cyclic rotation, full lips striking with quick repetition; engaging tight facial muscles, stretch, retreat, stretch, repeat. Mesmerized by the soft pink flush in her cheeks, passionate as she speaks, I tried to listen but I was lost in translation. I was rudely disrupted from my linguistic molestation by a rough slap on the back from Topher.

"Nice view, huh?" he grinned.

"Yeah, a lot going on. It's bad up in here. Nice atmosphere" I smiled. I tried to give him the non-sleazy bait, but he was not biting.

"Bullshit, you know I ain't talking about the atmosphere."

I actually had to laugh myself. "Sorry man, I ain't mad at'cha. You know." We clicked glasses, turned and leaned against the railing; Surrounded by natural beauty.

"So, you some kind of writer cat."

"Um, something like that." Not really sure where this is going, I strongly detest conversations that begin with "So...".

"You do alright with that?"

I breathed out slowly. "I guess. It keeps the cabinet full. Keeps me out of trouble, for the most part." I chuckle. Again, not knowing where this is going, I'm trying to keep this party polite.

"I mean, you out here rolling with the big dogs. I just, I thought maybe you wrote a bestseller or some Times top ten shit. I mean you set?"

"Man, this ain't exactly my bag bro'. I'm just here to support Kary. We go back, we cool. It's no sweat." I turn to watch the dance floor.

"I feel you man." Topher gestured toward me with a cigar.

I pat my pocket and pull out my cigarettes.

"Oh, Marlboro man." He snorted. I turn around, lean on the rail, reach for my Zippo, light my cigarette, inhale deeply and blow out slowly. As the Disc Jockey transitions track I hear a squeak, squeal, squawk. I look over my shoulder, Kary Parsons saw another long lost. I give a crooked smile, wink to the air and turn around, still smiling. I don't know the fuck why.

I feel Topher watching me. "So, you and Kary?"

I cut him off before the question gains hang time. "Just Friends."

"You know they got that bread though. I been hearing about the Parsons since I could say paid, publishing yo' joint, books and shit."

I shrug. He gives me a side glance and ashes on the floor.

"I'm not friends with her money", I replied with just a hint of snark. "It's got nothing to do with who we are, and it really makes no difference to me."

"Ah, see that's what I'm saying, you rolling like that? That shit ain't shit, huh Mr. Rockefeller?"

"You know." I pop my head a bit. I'm getting irritated, and I can get a little cocky when I'm irritated.

"I ain't mad'atcha. Go in for the booty and get the bounty." Topher cracks up Topher. For a big guy the evening's liquor toll was maxing for Topher. "I'm just saying ain't nothing partial about Kary

Parsons. She look like she tease a lil' bit though. 'Til a mother-fucker get serious; then a bitch a' learn. Maybe she'll learn tonight. A brother just might…"

"Er-hum." Joely is officially the best punch blocker I know. At that point I almost, I repeat almost, lost my damn cool. Considering myself somewhat of a wordsmith I rarely find the appropriate need for striking a "gentleman", but I will go monkey shit on a son-of-a-bitch. I was about to channel Uncle Roscoe on his ass.

"J-man" Topher spoke a little too loudly. "You set" he motion towards Joely's cup.

"Yeah, man." Joely shook the half-full glass.

"Walk with me." Topher gestured towards the patio area downstairs, and at the present moment, far away.

"Later" I raised my glass and lit another cigarette. Joely raised his eyebrows and nodded as they walked away.

They rest of the group convened and dispersed. I headed back to the veranda, and took in the solace of the night air, momentarily.

"Alright, alright, nephew. What it is, son?" Uncle Roscoe came in with a handshake, hug and a troop of delicacies. I got as far as Ginger and Lavender, rejuvenation and relaxation, respectively and respectfully. Uncle Roscoe wore rust-colored leather bell bottoms and a hypnotizing rust, gold, and brown wave of rayon large collared shirt – top three buttons undone to display a medley of thick gold chains and diamond encrusted medallions. Oh, and a full length Chinchilla. Roscoe's philosophy and I quote, 'winter, summer, spring or fall, you ain't never seen a fox with no fur at all.' I guess this was his spring coat. Hennessey in hands, Roscoe told me he had spent the evening in B.C.'s home studio. They were working on a new sound. Roscoe had the notion of putting spoken word to music, supplying a skillfully arranged beat and unleashing his creation onto the world. The music and entertainment industry was Roscoe's newest investment venture. I fixed a fresh drink to toast the occasion.

We were catching up on old times. The delicacies were catching up on new grinds, when a vision that was all fine stepped into the veranda.

"Look'a here, Look' a here" Uncle Roscoe was at full attention.

Madeline rushed onto the veranda, "I forgot my purse." She smiled and headed toward where we were seated.

"Roscoe, be cool, a lady on the premises."

Roscoe looked at me smiling. "Ol' Roscoe didn't get this far in school without no class." He dipped, walked over to Madeline, kissed her lightly on the hand and she responded with an er…big ol' bear hug! I guess there is something to be said for being covered in fur.

"Roy" she stood back and gazed at Roscoe.

"Bloom" He kissed her cheek. For the second time this trip I didn't even notice my empty glass.

"You've met…" half statement, mostly question.

"Oh, we go back a little." Madeline was all smiles linked arm in arm with "Roy".

Roscoe noted my shock er…surprise. "Abe, I am your mother's brother. This world ain't new culture."

"We met in college, right before graduation." Madeline assured. Roscoe went to college. Family History, damn. "Roy helped me find my voice."

I bet.

"Well, I better get back. Roscoe?" Roscoe promptly dismissed the delicacies and escorted Madeline back towards her villa, arm in arm like a gentleman, ever-so.

I, head shaking and smiling, waited a beat then headed back to the villa; what a night.

"This right here is where, is what happens when reason and opportunity meet; you know what I'm saying. These cats they got opportunities for no reason at all. Just be born and boom." I could smell the cigar smoke along the path, and just make out the voices of Topher and Joely. I wasn't intent on eavesdropping. My feet just kind of slowed their pace.

"You know my dad used to call my mom his little lamb. He would say she was all he ever needed. I used to want a little lamb and a modest income. We had enough. Until…" Joely trailed off.

"Until?" I could hear Topher pull on his cigar and exhale loudly.

"Until mom died and I moved to the Manor. Peter's place, well, his dad's at the time. Until then, it was just the place dad worked. He would come home some weekends, one week out of the month, and all summer when I guess, they travelled. We got lucky sometimes and he'd just show up during the week for no reason at all."

"Humph."

"I met Peter in the spring after mom passed, and Nyla that summer. I met her first, before Peter met her, I mean. She had been away at boarding school and stayed with relatives in Europe. The summer we met was her first home, full time. She lived in the neighboring estate. I wondered through her pasture one afternoon and there I found my honey blonde and tanned little lamb. I would sneak off every other afternoon to a world 'til then only imagined, into a persona invented and mastered to perfection, into amber eyes that danced like diamonds. She had no idea who I was, all that mattered was that I was. I lived in the right house. I wore the right clothes, spoke the appropriate language and lived vicariously through the right people. Our similarities were simultaneous. I could finish her sentences and describe places, people and events on cue. Our differences were dramatic, she made me feel like I had, and I made her feel like she wasn't lacking. Sometimes we would just sit in silence, and as the summer passed, she slowly let me in. I remember how the sunlight would dance along the angles of her face, how the starlight danced off the honey hued curls of her hair;

sometimes entangled and entwined, deep, deep in the meadow and the soft glowing light from the manor house served as a lighthouse beacon to the long slender miles to ecstasy. I surrendered. I told her truth and she helped me see the light."

"In my father's dying words, explaining why he wasn't there for mom as she lay slowly dying, he still served his master. He said, 'My son, life sometimes calls for difficult choices. Abraham would have surely sacrificed his son had God not sent a lamb." She led me to understand the how, she gave me the why. My honey blonde lamb was just enough. Then, I introduced her to Peter and the takeover began. Those amber eyes danced into diamonds, six carats to be exact. Peter got that I didn't have enough green pastures for her to feed on. And Peter, he wouldn't know modest if, well." Joely drifted in thought.

"Well, Joely this is your opportunity to have more than enough, huh." Topher nudged him and chuckled.

"I guess."

"Fuck that brother. After this you can buy a whole damn flock."

Joely paused in thought "Just one lamb Topher, just enough."

"You got to let the dough go to get the loaf of bread, brother."

"Tomorrow".

"Tomorrow".

I waited until I was sure they had drifted on, then quietly moved along to my villa. I entered quietly as possible, the only sound came from my rubber soled shoes as the squeaked on the slickly polished marble entry.

I had slept late and woke up feeling refreshed but parched. The smell of fresh coffee wafted across the downstairs living area and curled up the stairs with Sumatran aromatic promises of pleasure. I answer first nature's call, and then followed my nose to that dark mistress. Pouring her into a deep china vessel and introducing her to an even more seductive master who would forge the dark seas and drench my

dry palette, 'Hey Captain Morgan! Ahoy, my Caribbean oasis.'

Kary came in from the office area, alert and perky. "Thought

I smelled your standard IV." She sniffed the air, grabbed my cup and

took a long sip. "Hmm, Island coffee." She smiled. "I fired off a

letter to the Eden Club this morning. I figured they'd critique the

typeface, redesign the logo, and debate my controversial writing

style, all before getting down to club business, aka gossip." She

chuckled.

I laughed too, "In this group, Truth is a genre."

She bumped pass me as she headed to the patio area for a

swim in the sun warmed water of the private pool.

I refreshed my oasis, equal parts mistress and master and

followed her out. I thanked God for the strong spring sun, as a clever

ruse for my sun-glassed masquerade when she casually tossed the

sheer coverall on the lounger next to me and stepped into the clear

water. I supposed what she wore could qualify as a swimsuit in some

house of style. It could maybe even be categorized as a bikini if we go literally with fabric on the top and fabric on the bottom; and soft Bailey's Cream in all the places in between. If heat rises to the top, it serves to reason me burning my lips with steam from the coffee, as I absently lifted my cup to them in an effort to fill the gaping hole. She turned to me as she sank deeper into the water right down to that million dollar grin. Cha-mutha-fucking-ching.

"Careful, God might grant your wish to be a ripple." Jai snorted and punched me gently on the arm. "Door, wide open." She grinned.

"So, you came right on in?"

"Somebody's gotta be the aggressor."

"Subtle, Thor."

She plopped on the lounger. Jai wore a nice white jumper with bell bottom flare, a white straw fedora, cloth Mary Jane wedges, and killer Cat Eye shades. She just about looked like a girl.

"Coffee?"

Jai leaned over and sniffed. She didn't have to lean far. "Um, I'm good." She snorted and shook her head.

"Kary doesn't judge", I responded childishly with pouted lips spreading into a sheepish grin.

"Oh, un Lady Justice is a bit unbalanced in your court. You, my good man, for her, can do no wrong."

"Whatever" I retorted.

"You see it, we all do. Sadly, she's enamored, Chardonnay, when you clearly are in the mood for blackberry Merlot. Ah, the strength of ego that commands one to protect another with ferocity, even to damning consequence. It makes us believe that in others' weakness we have strength, without realizing until it is too late the fragility of the human heart. Ever was it to bear such burden. Think something that carries the heaviness of love can break easily under its strain; one must reinforce its walls if it is to remain of stone."

I had listened in silence. Put more "island" in my oasis, adjusted my shades in response, "There's the sunshine." I felt the now familiar Michigan chill still captured in the spring air, as Jai rose, waved hello/goodbye to Kary, punched me for good measure, and left the villa. She must have left the door ajar because I didn't hear it shut at her departure. No, it waited like a foreboding of the nights end, a gushing wind to come through, 'Door, firmly closed.'

I decided after that breath of fresh air to take a walk along the beach. We had been here almost two weeks. I was long overdue for a stroll, alone. I walk a lot back home. I unobtrusively observe people, taking in the sites, sights, and sounds of the city; noting interactions, reflecting, introspecting. Admittedly a little judging; and, if I wonder too far in varying directions, a little praying. Something about this place though, these people, the select, coveted few. Observant Abe was out of place and long overdue. This was admittedly foreign to me. I can't say when I last picked up a pen, or sat in contemplative thought. Maybe I feared taking it all in, what I would find, feared detaching…feared that I wouldn't fit back in again. I walked away from all this before, grew away from it to be honest, but familiar soil…

To live life in perpetual motion; I wondered if anybody here really thought, observed. If they really did exist beyond general awareness, of place, of things, or if they simply were, by being. Had I had a serious conversation that didn't feel ripped from a Gatsby-esque script, a melodrama? I'm being reflective because that's what my character would do, required dialogue to the big finale. This is the language of love. This is the speech of the privileged, and this, this is my heart breaking. At Eden Club we create stories, but I'd like to think we *live* life. There's planned moves, and plans of action but it's encased in raw feelings, sequences and consequences. Here, here is like a revolving stage. What really constitutes the end of the day? Nothing documented, noted, written or recorded, but life apparently happens here. And I, I guess am alive.

As if on cue, aligned with my thirst and the universe, dusk fell upon me and the Night Owl sailed into view. I walked with determined swiftness toward the docking sleek, black, killer whale of a yacht. As I approached the yacht I was surprised to see Madeline coming ashore. I guess her and "Roy" really were, are old chums. Definitely getting the dope on that from Unc'.

"Youngblood, what it is?" Uncle Roscoe, surprisingly, grabbed me in a huge bear hug.

"Alright, alright, nothing doing man, just taking a stroll and saw you pull in, so…"

"We ain't slow on the flow round here son, whiskey neat." Roscoe stayed in the know.

"Fo' sho''

He was already behind the bar. "What's on your mind? Speak it youngster." He smirked.

"Give me the damn drink Don Roy". I sipped, looked him over and we both chuckled. I refilled and tried to hold back the snickers 'cause Ol' Abe is just too funky to sip and spray.

Roscoe wore casual cream slacks and a linen cherry red madras shirt, a single gold braided chain, topped off with a tastefully designed – right I know, Roscoe – Red, Black and Green Kangol, soft cloth slip-on shoes of fine cherry red cotton with flexible rubber soles suitable for yachting. The last time I saw Roscoe decked in everyday I was blowing out six candles. Another notable, as I self-served my drink: no boat candy, or evening delights, and the young lady at the helm was Susan, just Susan. She had the nametag to prove it.

"Unc' on the real, what's good" I asked hesitantly, peering over the top of, okay hiding behind, my highball glass. I love my Uncle Roscoe dearly. But we both know I didn't know him well enough to be stirring in his Kool-Aid. Roscoe will let you know. "Hold that thought…"

"It's straight as a corner store weave nephew. Had a lil' business to attend to today, don't concern, don't concern. You know Roscoe got to go character and credentials on occasion."

"I dig Unc, I dig." I really wanted to ask about Madeline, but I felt I had already intruded enough. Roscoe and I were cool and I liked us just where we were. Sometimes you like the character just fine, you don't need to have a storyline. Just enjoy each prose, each fable, and treasure each moment as if it were the only one in time. Roscoe, me, was enough.

My uncle searched my face like only family can, shook his head and chuckled silently. "Nephew Abe, I see a kindred spirit in her. We spiritual soulmates, nuthin' more or less to it. We vibed

back then. And well, I rooted, and she bloomed. I watched her grow.

But like a dandelion. It can be a bright beautiful flower, but caught

in the wrong environment and lack of nurturing, that fragile flower

can become a weed. And any gust in the wrong direction can blow it

into a million parts. Scattered my bloom into little parts, one wish

per blow, each part granting them all to every stranger that picked

up. In a field of flowers surrounded by green, never seeing the

weeds, just this beautiful little thing. I tried man, but it was a

struggle. And Roscoe got to be Roscoe. And Roscoe don't struggle.

Some people shift to navigate through this world. She has that

ability. Me, I metamorphosized, to navigate this life." His eyes

misted. I lowered my gaze. He looked out of one of the large smoky

glass windows onto the life-giving, deep, baby blue, Michigan water.

Water that could nurture each bud, from root to petal. He whispered

into the room "Bloom my fragile flower. But should you start to

wither, and break into a million parts, know as you leave you take

but one from me, my heart." Roscoe shook the ice in his glass and I

shivered. He strolled to the bar and refilled his glass, extended the

bottle and topped of my whiskey. I learned from Roscoe: 'you don't get this far in school either by talking out of turn.' We finished our night cap in one swig of silence. I peace signed 'it's all good' and was out, heading back to Cornerstone. Yup, Roscoe and I were cool. I liked us just where we were.

I walked farther along the beach heading back to Cornerstone. I saw a light on at home base, aka Peter's Yacht. I thought I'd pop in and say 'Hey' to any and all aboard. I was also remembering that deep, beautiful dark mahogany wrap around bar, Top Shelf, for sure. As I padded along approaching the wooden oasis, I could hear voices, so, naturally, I slowed my stroll.

"Oh my God Nyla, Klaus, Buford Klaus Remington the Third," Kary at full vocal capacity. "For shit sake, they sell freaking retail, chain: door to fucking door. Oh God, I can't be retail! I can't be knockoff, I just won't!" Kary's voice was alarmingly stressed. I didn't think of girls like Kary for real stressed, you know. What the hell?

"Honey, KP," Nayla with her slight drawl. "At least you won't be wearing knockoffs. And who says you have to stay. Just give good face for a few years, secure your place and dip baby. Sweetheart, it's all for the greater goods." Nyla chuckled nervously. "Seriously though, sometimes KP: sometimes something has got to give. For us girls, this life won't last forever without guys like Klaus."

"Easy for you to say, your Klaus is freaking Peter, Sweetheart." Kary sniffled.

Nyla studied the pattern on her marble floor and tucked a stray strand behind her ear. "That doesn't mean a tough choice didn't exist. Don't be snarky because you're upset. Desperate and down and out are not synonymous. My point is, we need them. Kary, would your mama be doing this if we didn't? It might sound bitchy but sweetie, looks don't last forever. That's why we have daughters. Men like Peter, like your dad, they make it look easy and leisurely but it's not. That's why we woman accumulate, accommodate and procreate. It's harsh. It's truth, cold and hard, just like cash money. With any luck honey he'll get bored, and in the meantime, you stack sequential serial numbers, while he stacks model numbers." She actually laughed at her own joke.

But damn, this chick had prospecting down to a mutha'fuckin' science. I need a drink to tip to that. Kary breathed in hard and deep, and blew out so strongly it felt like I caught it mid-air, sucked it in and got knocked to my knees. Roscoe's words found the way back to me, 'I tried man'. But what could I do? What wasn't Kary telling me? Who the hell was Buford Klaus Remington, and why the hell would somebody Third that shit? Kary could work my nerves. But to hear the quiver, the uneasy resignation and well, fear, in her voice, I must admit, it kinda broke my heart. Kinda, right? My mind told me to quietly walk away, but the dry gully connecting my mouth to the back of my throat told me otherwise. Time to make my presence known.

"Hello, beautifuls." I flashed what I hoped was a refreshing, room illuminating, mood ring altering, kilo-watt grin.

"What's up Abe?" Nyla was already behind the bar.

"Nuthing, just rolling through from Uncle Roscoe's." Good God, I'm making this yacht hopping thing sound normal.

"Oh, well we were just girl timing it. Peter's not here, some clandestine meet-up. Clandestine because he felt the need to make up the town: Kalamazoo. Yea, okay Petey, that's real." The sarcasm dripped like water droplets on a glass of cold iced whiskey in warm hands.

I sipped my drink and searched Kary's face. She could dry the tears, but the pink tipped nose was a dead give-away. I thanked Nyla for the 'cool drank' and asked if they were heading back to the villas. Nyla said she was going to stay on the yacht for the night, so Kary and I left her in the gentle waves of the arms of Lake Michigan.

Kary was uncharacteristically quiet so I prodded gently. "Everything cool?" I rubbed my hand gently down her arm and pulled her closer.

She shrugged in, "Copasetic."

"One more time with conviction" I nudged playfully.

She responded with more silence. I thought maybe I could spark her with some of her favorite, gossip, or as she says, information exchange.

"411 operator." I made the universal head mic adjustment signal. She shook her head. "Come'on, Kary."

She smiled and made the universal fist to ear, thumb and pinky extend headset sign "Um'er yeess."

I mocked: "Information calling, honey."

We both giggled. She said, "What?"

I smiled and pinched her cheek. "See. Look here, did you know Madeline was cool with my Uncle Roscoe, like way back cool?"

"Your Uncle Roscoe, Power to the People Roscoe, oh, oooh."

Kary had met Roscoe briefly when he rolled through town about a year ago around my birthday. He thought she was just the type of gusty wind I needed. The problem with wind gusts is they are meant to shake things up for a moment and then blow on by. And in Roscoe's book of love, that's just enough.

"That Roscoe." She recovered.

"Yes," and I quoted " 'God Bless America and Dr. King, cause you's a beautiful product of the melting pot, sweet thing', Roscoe." I cracked up. "Yeah, I know right. You remember that."

"Damn fool, who would forget it." She smiled. I tried man, and thought I had succeeded in lightening her mood. But…well, "That's Madeline for you." She mumbled.

She seemed somewhat less somber for the wear. "Full of surprises. But I guess you have to have that shifting ability, to fit in anywhere. Money may get you there, but it takes a lot more to keep you there. Especially the places we go."

I gave her an 'er' look. "What's that supposed to mean? She's got money, means, obviously beautiful and a sweet, swell, smart personality. What gives?"

"Whatever, did that come on the fan club flyer in the back of your highlights magazine? I'm just saying, well, like Nyla and I. People – we look like – well, we fit in without any accouterments. So I get it for Madeline. It's just, some of us don't have to try so hard." She was getting snarky.

"I wouldn't say Madeline has to try at anything" I snarked back. I was going from sympathetic to irritated. Not "oh Kary works my nerves irritated" but pissed-offedness irritated. Kary can be judgmental like most privileged folk but this was literally going to a dark place. And Abe don't get down like that.

"Oh stop getting defensive about your precious Madeline. I'm just stating a fact. I'm not socially blind to any advantages, economic or otherwise. I guess to put it in conscious terms, if I'm alone or with Nyla, I don't necessarily have to worry about the proximity of my seat to the kitchen; or the entrance I use. Is that clearer for you?" Her behavior was quite unbecoming and becoming an issue for me.

"What the hell has gotten into you? Madeline's our friend!" She was about to make me start raising me voice, and that's something my cool queue just don't generally allow.

"Friend, fucking friend, you just met the bitch. Oh are you blindsided by her wealth and beauty and oh, I'm so Miss Soul like everybody else. Whatever Abe, I thought you were different. Nyla's right. Can't do different. If you want fresh bread go to the baker not the butcher, there all you get is fresh meat."

"Is that the issue Kary? Dough, literally, cause Madeline can make her own choices, cause she owns the baker and the recipe – you just know where to shop." Zing mutha' fucking Zing, and yes, that shit felt good.

"You know what Abe?"

"What?" Damn, I got so caught up I answered a rhetorical.

"Fuck you, that's what. You go be enamored, what do you care? You're happy with nothing, and nowhere and someone who can't take you anywhere near the levels somebody like me," She stumbled over the next sentence, "or whoever can. Is that what you want, Afro-Chic? I hope Topher breaks her heart and I hope she rips yours apart!" She was a slobbering mess, shaking and fiercely fighting back tears.

"Kary, Enough!" I did raise my voice for that one. I reached out and put her face in my palms. I felt her tremble and the hot tears rolled from her eyes and cheeks onto my hands and down my wrists. They left a moist tear-streaked trail all the way down my forearm. I kissed her gently on the forehead. "Enough."

She spoke gently and with considerably more calmness. She sniffled through her words. "That's the problem Abe, it's going to say on your tombstone, 'Here Lies Abe, The cat who saw all and had enough.' But, but..." She broke down sobbing, "But it's not Abe, it can't be." She choked back saliva and saline-doused liquid pain. "If only thinking made it so." She stood up straight, and fingered combed her sun-kissed highlighted hair. The shine in those emerald eyes darkened, like lights out in the mine. The sweet bird is out of breath. "Goodnight Abe."

I reached out to her "Kary, I can't let you go like this, I'll walk you back. You shouldn't be alone." I held onto her arm.

She shook her head and pulled away. I let her go, but somewhere in Kary-Land her universe was letting her down and breaking her heart. I knew she needed time. And I well, for what I hope is clear and obvious reasons this time, needed a drink, for real. I headed over to the cigar lounge.

The cigar lounge evening atmosphere was a dimly lit montage of expensive smoke, mellow tobacco and an even more mellow jazz, Miles Davis in current rotation. Encased within the dark cherry wood walls and deep emerald and golden marble tiled floors, one could experience camaraderie, friendship, fellowship and the only females allowed in (except Jai, or course)…servers fine as hell. A soft smile spread across my face as I headed to the bar. The deep tan blinds were up exposing a beautiful view of the lake that seemed to stretch into infinity. Relaxation and life transcending into eternal bliss; easy, smooth and nary a wave. If only thinking made it so. The moonlight shining in the window waltzed with the amber liquid in my glass offering a melodic trance and promise of peace, serenity, calmness, and undiluted tranquility. I moved to find a comfortable, quiet place and sank slowly into the plush ruby leathered sofa. I watched crystals sparkle under the Tiffany lighting like a million icy dollars. They reminded me of a grin that had come to grow on me. I held the glass for comfort, consumed the liquid with love. The irony was not lost. I took in the solace of the quiet corner to brood over the events of the day. I had barely perfected my pout when the brooding silence was breached. In hindsight I was glad for the company. I've never been one for sinking into a depressive stupor. My eyes met sharp wing tipped dark green leather platforms, peeking out underneath deep green trousers. I smirked and let my eyes take the 'slow boat to china'; all the way up every dip and curve of the miles and miles of great gammed wall. Right into deep brown eyes glaring with sarcastic menace, shadowed underneath an Evergreen, perfectly placed fedora with a dark gold and green snake skin band. My apologetic eyes might have been convincing if they weren't still taking the scenic route over the sleeveless polyester golden belted tunic parting its buttoned embrace right at seated eye level to reveal exquisite landscape and Peking mountain peaks that could have only been formed by the hand of God. I swallowed hard and tried again to cue up shame and humility required by those partial to the movement.

"Oh please" Jai snickered. "Nobody believes that shit on the Geisha and they sure as hell don't believe it from you."

"Touché" I motioned for her to join me.

Though she smelled heavily of bourbon and Chanel No. 5, she sat down Tequila Sunrise in hand. She signaled to the server, whom had apparently been waiting in the wings, and he promptly deposited a whiskey on the rocks and eight shots of Cuervo. Jai leaned back, crossed her legs and smiled.

"Damn."

"Damn right." She replied. Jai leaned forward, separated her knees, rested an elbow to knee, leaned in and nodded towards the aligned shots. She hadn't said much and needn't say more. We knocked'em back 1-2-3-4-5-6…Seven, Eight. She circled in the air, and duplicate set appeared. She giggled as we paced this round.

"I know I come here because I love that I'm the only girl who can; but what's your excuse? I figured you more for fresh air pep, veranda. Not sulky, somber, dark wood paneled rooms."

"Not so much tonight, I guess."

She leaned back and smirked. "Hmmm, finally seeing the true colors of Cornerstone; not all Red, Gold, Green and Cream? The nary-a-care of luxuriate indulgence and entitlement sure does tend to bring out the natural being don't it."

I nodded in agreement and exhaled.

"It's easy when they tell you that you have it all." She shrugged, "But better when you figure it out for yourself."

"More being, less beast, all true essence. Dig?"

"Dig."

We toasted our last shot. I shook my glass for a refill, she offered up hers as well.

Once we were freshened up, she was the first to break the silence. "What's up bro? What's with the gloom and doom for real? You look like you need to get your solid back." Her voice was deep and throaty with drink as she absent-mindedly toyed with her belt. Her crossed leg mesmerized with a slow winding bob.

I shook my head slowly, and nursed my drink. I know right. I wanted to ease into this, whatever this was. I sat up and rubbed my thigh in contemplation.

"I make you nervous?" Her deep mauve colored lips pursed into a smile of cool, confident comfort. She tilted her head and smiled.

I smiled back. "Nah, no that's not it. I'm just trying to figure, figure you out." She laughed out loud.

"Why, cause I don't fit the gig?"

"Something like that. You're so much more. I mean, you're heavy man. So, why do this, all this."

She winked. "I do me Abe. I'm a complex matrix, in a world whose pattern I recognized, a universe I can maneuver and not get lost. It was a long time coming and hard lessoned learned. I've had my reflective moments. I've seen what this world can do without even going beyond the walls of my supposed shelter. I made my decision to navigate within this designated space, for my allotted time, in peace. I can control neither what people think nor do. I can only control how I let it affect me. In that way, this life is the life for me: self preservation, a game by any other name, baby."

"That's deep."

"No, deep my friend, is the shit hole you stand in until what they dump on you is high enough for you to climb out."

I realized that the difference was I never really felt dumped on. So shit hole was unfamiliar territory. And though I don't think I was there yet, downwind wasn't a place to be either. I think she read the contemplation in my face.

Jai leaned forward and patted my knee. "Dumped on is relative. Sometimes it's seeing things you never really wanted to. Or realizing things you just wish didn't surface, like the truth."

I nodded once again, in agreement.

She snickered. "Dude, man. On a lighter note, a true note if you will, this right here: Cornerstone, my friends, it's just pure entertainment." She squealed, squeaked, and squawked. We both broke out in laughter. It felt good. "Look man, dig this, I'm amused. You know what I'm saying. I'm just on the outskirts enough to slip away unnoticed when I need to, when I have to. We do what we do to maintain. It's easier for some than for others. Don't make it bigger than it has to be babe." She signaled to the server and ordered bourbon tall and me whiskey to suit. She leaned in, "Go home Abe, this isn't you. It won't be. If I knew a cat could grow up in this world and turn out like you…well." The corners of her eyes glistened in the dim room, she blinked them wide and her lips formed a thin self forgiving smile.

I touched her nose. The bourbon would play a remorseful melody if you wrote the notes. She winked and leaned back. We sipped in silence. A little more collected she spoke. "We're here because here is the train stop to the next there. I hang out to recharge, live wire feed. Then, as I've learned, I unplug, go away and ride out the charge. I used to be like Nyla, like Kary, even like you. But I had to find a middle ground. Once I did, I marketed that line to myself and bought every fucking product it made."

"The thing is Abe, people with infinite means, money and, or power are different. Being more means being in their environment. I say their environment because, because of their resources they make any place their own; conducive to them and their needs. That's never going to change. But we do. People like us, we can be the difference makers. You can make changes that affect the environment literally and physically or you can change the world. We each do our part, consumer or contributor. Right now, you are being a chameleon. When was the last time you wrote or did the things you tell us about at your Eden Club. Chameleons hide Abe, hide, change to fit in. Even from the little I know, I know that's not you. You have a greater power. You create worlds, don't give up in this one."

She was right. I usually write or pontificate daily. But here, until today, I had not. I was changing in this brief time. It was all consuming. But then again, she was wrong. I shouldn't go home. I can dig this. I'm way too funky to not ride this out.

"I'm just saying," she continued. "You do things that let you know amidst all the intricacies of this you're still in there. I think for people like you and me, those little things, writing, observing, music, whatever, keep our consciences aware and alive. And if we stop, it's clear we are being slowly consumed. We don't necessarily get overwhelmed, but we're taking so much in. In an effort to understand, we become. For us, the new awakening if not a refresh, is a digression. Where your conscience goes Abe...Morality is sure to follow."

I scratched my temple, sat back and drained my glass. Getting to know this side of Jai was refreshing and I felt like I could trust her, and her opinion. I don't know, as these words found the way to me 'I saw a kindred spirit.' "Can I ask you something Jai?"

"Anything you want babe." She leaned back and listened.

"Kary. I think she's got something going on. I mean, she doesn't usually get really rattled. But she was tonight. You know, she just start dogging Madeline. Harping on who had what, and implying that, well like it was wrong for people to want something different. Like what we're talking about now. Wrong to want different than," I gestured around the room, "all this."

Jai nodded.

I knew I was rambling a little, but it felt good to talk to someone that maybe could see through it all, and maybe make sense of it with me. I continued, "And well, she made some unfair comparisons to looks and advantages, that were quite frankly uncharacteristic of her to me. I don't know maybe that's her bag around you guys. But I, you know. It's just not…"

She interrupted, "Your Kary."

I sigh out my frustration. Not this again. "Whoa, partner."

She got it. "I mean, just, whatever, forget it."

The words know and love crossed my mind; strangely reminded me I needed to piss. "Hold that thought." I handled the business. I watched Jai at our table as I made my way back through the crowed small space just past the late night impromptu jam session. Some of the musicians from the grandstand show had stopped in and, as a musician will tend to, just pulled out instruments and let it do what it do.

Jai took off her hat and shook out her long black hair, waves fell gently around her face. In the dim corner lights it reminded me of the soft moonlight catching shadows of bodies and dark sheets. Where instead of getting out of bed you just give the sheets a good fluff, they catch in the cool breeze from an open bedroom window, and then fall gently again atop the souls eager to intertwine. She caught my eye and pushed the soft waves underneath the hat and gave the fedora a firm tug, setting it low once again. I sat down to a fresh drink, she was back on the Tequila Sunrises. Smiles all around.

"So..."

"So Abe, you're what's going on with Kary." She clarified. "KP comes from a place where security is everything. When it feels like its slipping away, well difficult choices have to be made. More so, reality sets in, the truth hurts when shit gets real. Even though it feels like you would die without someone, love and survival don't always go hand in hand. Some people strike out when they can't control or manipulate the environment we talked about, and they feel like other people don't have to make choices, whose worlds are never threatened. Madeline has learned to adapt, and navigate like me, but in a different way. So still like them, her environment never really has to change. To Kary, navigation, adaptation, money does that for her. When she has to take an active, human hand in things, well she can't. She doesn't know how, not yet. That kind of legacy takes time; time to hone those survival instincts to kill." She chuckled.

I did not.

"Look babe, her world is falling apart, maybe you can help A.B.E, maybe you can't, but you need to talk to her. Find her motivation. Find out if you can be honest, truthful. Find out if love is enough. Whatever y'all's deal, find her measure of enough, and yours."

The server interrupted briefly to clear our growing collection of crystal. So as not to appear to have lost our appreciation for the finely cut stone, we ordered a set of eight. We thought it only fair to let the light dance with the facet shaped vessels so we quickly removed the obstructing liquid in the first four she set down. I lit a Marlboro and Jai's cigar. We continued the conversation.

"You know the whole Madeline thing, well that is unfortunate. But don't judge KP by it. Unfortunately it's the backlash of our lack of understanding of the chaos in our lives. To cope sometimes we create a chaos we can manage. The confusion of race, tone and privilege is a created chaos that we can manage, a justification for behavior or lack thereof. For those out of control, manufactured justice far out balances a universal, cosmic one, like that bitch is just naturally better than you."

We do both chuckle and fist bump to that.

"Hmm. Cosmic chaos, versus crafted chaos; you rocked out. It just got serious up in here."

We each swig a shot.

"You got a groovy way of making sense girl." I smiled and she toasted.

"To groovy points all around." We stood, stretched.

"Talk to KP Abe, for real though. Well, I gotta push off. I think I've hid from Mortimer long enough. Every now and then I got's to duck out of dorkville county."

"Aww man, he's a cool cat." I punch her lightly.

"You're a cool cat." She punched back, but hard.

"I know that, but he is cool."

She dropped her head in a shy crooked smile and a wink, "I know that."

Now, I'm way too cool and waaay too funky to point out to her the look of love. Way too funky for that. I knew I should go check on Kary. I did hate seeing her like that, literally and figuratively. I ordered a couple of shots of good idea or not's to help me decide.

Full of liquid courage and care I headed towards the villa to check on Kary. As I approached I heard the click clank of her typewriter as the sound carried through the open window. I stood outside and lit a cigarette, inhaled and waited.

"Go away Abe." A sharp voice echoed from the small room.

"Om Kary" I responded.

"Wha? Don't oh Kary me Abe."

"I said, OM, O-M Kary."

"What the heck is Om Kary?"

"I'm trying a subliminal calming technique; Om instead of 'Oh' or 'Oh, my' in response to someone else's tension filled retorts.

It's a subtle message to relax, take it down a notch, you know…chill." I made smoke rings to accentuate my point.

"Yeah, how's that working out then?" I could sense the laughter in her tone. I thought to myself, cha-ching, i-ching. Okay, maybe going a little too far, I know. I stood silent for a moment.

"Go away Abe."

"Okay, but only if you admit my OM Kary worked out the sidecar of bitter in your tone." I peaked in the window and saw a smile slowly spreading across her face as she peeked from the corner of her eyes. I blew hot air on the window and wrote O – M on the glass. She finally looked full on in my direction and pointed sharply; her smile slowly graduating into a grin. I'd take a million dollar loan out against that and give her time.

I decided to hang out on the veranda until bedtime or least until I was too tired to care, to care about Kary Parsons. Too tired to wish I was back at Eden Club, back in my room overlooking New York City streets, where give a damn was in the details; where nobody has time for that.

Topher, Madeline and Joely were all on the veranda.

"Champagne, what did I miss?" I stepped into the area and greeted them, feeling slightly underdressed. I hadn't changed since my walk on the beach. Still in my cotton button-up, cotton undershirt and dark cream cargo pants. I had gotten the pants on a trip to South America for a photo essay on the burgeoning interest in the healing plants and properties of the rainforest. It was theoretically a tourist-oriented, camping tours propaganda type piece, nothing too deep. I got a few looks, either because nobody wears cargo pants, or probably more likely here, because they were made for labor, not label made.

"Abe, come over, grab a glass." Madeline's eyes danced with glee. She looked dazzling in a red Halston tank dress that was so close to see-through that I had to self-check imagination versus real deal. She had her hair in two puffs, each tied with golden tassels and gold glitter around her dark green eye shadow. The dress contoured with deadly accuracy. As I got close, I didn't have to imagine much at-tol.

"Celebrating?" I kissed her lightly on the cheek in greeting and reached for a glass. I motioned towards Joely and Topher and sat down to join the group.

"Yes! Madeline squealed. "And you can keep me company while these two dialogue about their business deal."

I caught the flash of Topher's quick look at Madeline. A look that said 'I see two afro-puffs but I'm hearing blonde,' a look that let me know, to let it pass.

I quickly clasp Madeline's free hand and gave it a little shake. "Hey, I'm hanging in suspense here, what's up?" Madeline, all smiles, wiggles, and giggles held up an official looking piece of paper, guessing by the gold-embossed letterhead.

Shaking it about two inches from my eyes she shrieked, "Read it, Read it!"

I reached for the paper and gave her a smile. Her excitement was contagious and intoxicating. Apparently it was from Parsons Publishing House. The letter announced that they would be publishing Madeline's collection of poetry. Madeline had been writing poetry and submitting her work to contests and for various anthologies since college. But this would be a complete book, a solo effort showcasing her work.

"Congratulations, you will be immortalized!"

She leaned in and hugged me tight. Topher and Joely rejoined our little twosome. "Yes, lil' Ol' me. I'm so excited. It's the literary equivalent of shouting from the rooftop, I have arrived!!"

"Proud of you sista', you hit the mark." Joely tipped his glass with sincerity. He smiled and kissed her on the forehead. We signaled the waiter for some real drinks.

"Oh, Joely. I feel like it's time. We've been working so hard; and like you. You have this thing with Topher and you can finally be…" Topher shot her another look; the glider will soar forever on the hang time of the un-ended statement after Topher's glare. Madeline shimmied her shoulders,

"Well, I feel like I should toss you a bouquet like at a wedding; for luck, to make sure you're next." She grabbed a handful of white lilies from the vase on the table; loosed and freed one of the golden tassels on her puffed ponytail and tied it around the bunch of flowers. "Okay ready, to our moment to leave a mark on this world, our season." With that she turned around on the couch, with her back to Joely and tossed the tasseled white lilies over her head. They caught in the wind and the loosely tied binding came undone, just as Joely reached up. Eight white lily with green stems gathered in the air floated slowly down around us. One caught up further in the gust, went over the rooftop veranda, and down into the crystal pool below.

Topher poured the last of the champagne into his glass. He turned the flute up to his lips. "Ah, the world according to Madeline. You deserve it babe." He finished every last drop.

Madeline looked into his eyes, gave a slight head tilt and followed suit. I sat the letter down and asked her to walk me through her fairytale.

Giles entered the veranda announcing a telephone call for Topher. Topher accepted and waited for Giles to connect the call by the bar.

"Er-hum" Joely excused himself and nervously paced the parameters. Okay.

As Madeline and I were talking Nyla stepped onto the veranda, "Hey Ya'll!" She looked much more at ease than she did earlier in the day. She wore a cream colored close fitting Oscar De'La Renta caftan and soft cream colored wedge sandals. On her ears were large diamond encrusted hoop earrings. In the air, dirty martini. "Congrats Madeline, I guess news travels fast. Peter's not back yet so I figured I would stop over and share in your moment."

Madeline smiled and handed her a glass of the freshly arrived Dom Perignon. I wasn't sure but the air seemed heavy with tension or envy, kind of like I sensed from Kary earlier. I was so not in the mood. One would think her long time friends' enthusiasm would match her efforts. I personally could not have been happier for Madeline. I learned from her the nature of her visit to Roscoe earlier. She wanted to tell him first about the publishing deal and gain his approval to include him in her dedication, ever mindful of his rep amongst his cohorts. Roscoe, of course, gave it five – on the Black Hand side. It couldn't hurt to lend credibility to his ever-expanding empire either.

"Hey, Hey now, what it do baby girl." Jai and Mortimer filed in tossing confetti.

Mortimer melodically chimed in "You can tell everybody!" with a soul-filled twist.

Madeline was full of champagne and excitement. "Let me show you the written proof that I artistically arrived. Oh, let me fill glasses first."

As she poured Topher was finishing up his phone call. "Yeah, yeah, let me note that."

I watched in torrid shock as Topher leaned and reached for the paper on the table, looked at it, snorted, turned the paper word side down and proceeded to 'note' whatever 'that' was on Madeline's announcement. All over Madeline's letter from the publisher, black marks across her happiness, hopes and success; and undoubtedly her self-esteem. Metaphor abounds. We all watched in silence. Madeline's eyes glistened in the flickering light from the candle centerpiece. She reached up to Topher for the document.

"I'ma need t'hold this for a minute. Give it to you in the room." She looked at him wide-eyed. He gave a kiss in her direction and said, "You don't need this piece of paper to show you what I already know. You're the best." He shrugged. "Just celebrate baby girl. Celebrate." With that he tucked the letter into his breast pocket. For a guy who makes a living as a writer and a woman who just got a book published, we were collectively at an amazing loss for words.

I gently reached out and touched her knee, smiled awkwardly and headed for the bar.

Jai came over for a mixed drink. "You talk to KP?" I shook my head. "Nah, she seemed alright, so I figured I'd let her be for a while." We just sipped in the silence of the moment.

Nyla casually strolled over to the bar. "Hey Abe, give me a couple of shots. I guess in honor of the occasion, make it something dark." She giggled. I could smell clearly how she had spent her alone time on the yacht.

Jai looked her over, "Nyla, stop."

Nyla gave her a light shove and swayed at the bar. "Whatever! The only reason that damn book got published is because the Parsons Publishing House is struggling tooth and nail to stay relevant. What better way to stay with the times than to mass print for the cliché of the day. Every negro out here is a poet, unsung hero for the movement, revolutionary visionary." She ranted, drink in hand.

"Okay!" Jai gently removed the glass from Nyla's hand and pushed the spare towards me. "Time-to-go" she said firmly.

Joely had made his way to the bar, sparked by the commotion. "Peter back yet?"

"No" Nyla replied. "I'm staying at the yacht til' he returns; but I'm headed to Kary's right now," she slurred. "I just stopped here on the way. I didn't want to be rude."

"Maybe you should have shot for a less lofty goal." Mortimer murmured. Jai nodded towards him and he gently took Nyla's dangling free arm and the gently shoved, er, escorted her from the veranda.

Topher tapped Joely on the shoulder and patted his sport blazer, top pocket and whispered, "12 n 12 bro; Gonna need an answer."

Joely nodded "24 hours, got it." Joely exited behind Nyla and company with Nyla reciting very, very bad poetry down the hall.

"Whew" I exhaled loudly and slammed back Nyla's lonely shot. Topher and Madeline were talking quietly in the corner. I overheard a few laughs and giggles so I guessed all was good.

Jai came back around and sat down exasperated. "I could no longer endure the prose of Nyla Rose" she spoke into the smoke of her freshly lit thin cigar.

"Yeah" I shook my head. "Rare form, right; what you drinking?"

"Chivas." I poured.

Jai snuggled into the egg shaped barstool and raised her glass in a toast, "Welcome to the ninth and final layer my friend." The glasses clicked together and the overflowing amber liquid inside danced in perfidious repose.

"What the heck tho', man? It's like all this celebrating for Madeline set off some brewing tension from hell." I freshened our drinks and leaned in as Jai motioned me closer. Madeline and Topher were still talking in the distance, no point in ruffling additional feathers this evening.

Jai proceeded in explanation. "Truth is Kary, and you really should talk to her by the way, is trying to secure her future for lack of better terminology. Nyla was correct somewhat in that the Parson Publishing House is struggling to stay afloat in terms of relevance and attracting today's audience. But they are a staple and they will bounce back. I think though this little setback serves as an uncomfortable reminder that promises don't guarantee place. Legacy and inheritance can be a house of cards. I'm sure Mr. Parsons has some legal protection for Kary financially. But with families as old as ours we've all heard the horror stories of families wealthy in name only. I think Mom P is pushing Kary to gain her own security. And not to be snarky, but heaven forbid she actually work for it in the traditional sense."

I nodded, "Well now, that clarifies something I got wind of earlier. Humph." I thought to myself maybe I wasn't so different. If my foot slipped into this ninth level would it be so wrongly placed. To each their own, as the end justifies the means.

"What?" Her eyes glistened in the light with girly gossip glee; Kind of a funny look on Jai. Brooks Brothers would not be glee-lighted.

Well, what they hell, I was in. "I overheard Nyla say something along those lines to Kary, before the marathon meltdown. Something about Klaus Remington the..."

"Third" she finished my sentence. "Yeah, brutal shit right there. Well Nyla would know, she was in a similar stitch, but…"

"Her Klaus was Peter. Yeah, that was the fire that lit the icecap." I finished her sentence.

She absently rubbed her thigh and smiled. "That's really what set them off about Madeline. Really, usually, mostly it's all cool. It's just when their little worlds are lit by anything other than the bling of shiny things. They revert to old bad habits, status, race, you know. And they don't see how Madeline is accepted everywhere she goes, makes friends, loyal friends, easily, people assume her wealth. They think their bourgeoisie gets them in the door, and it does. But people can also see girls like them coming a mile away. They see the bitch or brat or inheritance bait or any combination of such, as they are. To try to explain personality or character to them is a lost cause. It's all reputation: who you know and what you have. Everything else, everyone else, is what can you do for me category; Upstairs, Top Shelf or non-existent: simple and American as apple pie."

"'And they call it paradise, I don't know why…'" Jai smiled and half the freshly prepared dirty martini disappeared down her throat. "You know, the issue too is, that Madeline's money is her own. Although she has family money, she's amassed a small fortune of her own, through hard work, and again friendships. Aunts and uncles with whom she nurtured relationships on her own. But, like I said, through hard work too. I think it makes them a little envious. But you know for Kary and Nyla, it's that Madeline can marry for love. I mean she is really alright on her own. Like for me, I can walk away. I mean, I know my family's money isn't going anywhere, but I also don't care. Working and striking out to make my fortune, if you will, is character building; and can only ensure that what I do get, any way I get it, lasts for generations too. Don't get me wrong though bro', I likes a solid foundation from which to build." She chuckled through that one. "And although coming here, to Cornerstone was my way of showing the 'rents I'm back in the fold. Abe, I'm always going to be headstrong and independent. I know I can be successful and financially sound on my own. I ventured out and tried. I proved to myself that I could. Besides, I'm way too funky not to hold my own."

I laughed out loud and toasted, "Kin."

"Kin" she toasted back.

Jai and I had not noticed that Topher and Madeline had slipped off.

"Oh man." Jai jumped off the barstool. "Dude, I gotta kick bricks. Mortimer and I are supposed to be going site seeing for artistic inspiration. I figured I help him enough with his geek sheik shit so turnabout is fair play. Early start tomorrow. She put up a fist, I half bowed. She dropped three digits and a thumb, and used the remaining to tug down the fedora strategically, ever-so.

I figured Kary had enough alone time and Nyla time, Lord please. So I should be good with a night cap and maybe, maybe coffee and a friendly cozy fire. Maybe even some good ol' fashioned Eden Club talk time; just me and Kary Parsons; my Kary Parsons, or so the mind decided. As I neared our villa, I saw Nyla walking towards me. I had already chopped her earlier comments up to the dwellings of the ninth circle and chosen to forgive and forget. My attitude adjustment was a good thing because as we met on the brick pathway she hugged me close and tight. I know now isn't the time.

But I was surprised by the smoothness of her contours and malleability of her slender, toned French vanilla cream flesh; the pertness on high, and mine just below as the hug lingered slightly shy of the opposite of sobering.

"Nyla" I forced a, in full disclosure, leer into a smile and held her back at, let's just say, arms length.

"Abe" she held her head in her hands shook out the cobwebs. Then she placed both hands on my chest and looked up at me with a crooked smile and wiggled her upped half from side to side.

"Yeess?" I held her again, at arm's length.

She cast her eyes downward, hesitated and spoke. "I, well, I'm not apologizing, cause I was, well, mad. So fair is fair." She questionably stated with a pout. Well I guess logic and Hennessy don't mix, but okay. I matched her crooked smile, cause, well, she was sexy as hell, without any liquor or logic or fairness at all. I kissed her lightly on the cheek, linked arm in arm and agreed to her request to walk her back to home base. We enjoyed the walk and night air together.

She leaned her head on my shoulder as our steps fell in sync. "Abe" she hesitated.

"Yeesss?" Again.

"I need a favor." No hesitation, just rapid fire. "You seem like, well, you're really good with people. I mean, you lead a club and all. You've gotten to know us all pretty well, so I feel confident in asking, and because I'm worried. I don't know who else could help."

I stopped to listen and slow her down. "What do you need Nyla?"

I was sobering up fast and didn't particularly care for it. Besides my heart was progressing slowly towards my throat remembering she had just spent the evening with Kary. I didn't want to care that deep, but I did. I didn't want to give what I couldn't take back, and I didn't want...this, to get ahead of myself. So I tracked back to my original intent; stop and listen.

"Abe, I need you to talk to Joely. He's kind of come out of his shell around you. Believe it or not, it's possible for him to interact less. Point is, I think that Topher is pulling him into something, and I don't think it is something that he should be doing. I think his motives are all wrong. Not from a bad place just wrong."

"Topher, ya' damn skimpy, believe it."

She chuckled, "I actually meant Joely. Of course I don't trust Topher. I mean why Joely, why now? Those two have never been particularly close. I think he is taking this vacation as an opportunity to slip in between Peter and Joely. When new enterprises go up, that's akin to blood in the water for Peter. His opportunity to learn everything he can, spot the weakness and position himself as close to the proverbial juggler as possible; just-in-case. Abe, I just need you to see if this is legit. I can't, it's too complicated, history and all. But I care about my friends. I love them and protect them fiercely, even if it is from themselves. Her fist were white-knuckled, neither of us had realized how tightly she clutched my shirt. She looked down at her balled hands clinched in the gathering fabric, let go and smoothed down my shirt as a gesture.

I held both her hands, "I know. And all is fair in love. I will talk to him. But let me ask, have you talked to Peter? I mean surely Joely would listen to him well before he would even talk to me. If he's not talking to Peter, honey..." I thought I would try to caution her.

"But that's my point. I think this is emotion driven. I think Joely thinks that he has options of things or persons that he doesn't. I think he thinks that he is doing something that will yield him results and outcomes that aren't going to happen."

"Do you mean you?" I had to ask. I was getting thunked out and thirsty.

"We have old history. I made my choices. And Joely doesn't have, and will never acquire, what it takes to change them."

"Let me guess, whatever he does, it won't be enough." I folded my lips in a thin affirming line.

"It won't be Peter." She stated.

"Enough said." I held her gaze.

She pressed her lips together in finality. The tears that threatened the rim of her eyes as she pleaded earlier, chilled to a glisten against the cool Michigan night air. I pulled her close and kept my arm around her all the way to home base.

We had further to go than we realized so to fill the time and block out the breeze as we got nearer to the lake, Nyla gave me a little history lesson. I nodded and listened with pensive silence. It pretty much aligned with what I overhead Joely telling Topher.

From Nyla's perspective I gained insight into the ending. "Abe, I just knew I didn't want to live out my life waiting for a big break. Somebody to die, a hand me down fortune, to piecemeal out success and opportunity as it suited them; or be a charity case. I didn't want to ever risk being an observer, on the outskirts, just within reach. Or worse to have tasted it all my childhood and spend my adulthood savoring the flavor of past decadence. I wanted to keep it, have it, up close and personal access, always. It sounds shallow, I know. But look it, I didn't want to be one of those people that has to be nice to everybody because I don't know who I will need down the line, who could help me or who I could use. Those,

those are the truly shallow, Abe. Me, I'm just honest. At the end of the day Abe, what the money really provides is the choice to be honest, to be real, the comfort to care or not. With Peter I don't have to make apologies, excuses, or judgments. I know there's people that come into my life with motives like those I mentioned. But since I know that, I don't have to worry. I can be friends for friends' sake, and be done for goodness sake, just as I damn well please. Isn't that what everyone is fighting for anyway?" She paused in thought, then spoke. "It's not that I didn't love Joely, Abe. It's that I didn't want Joely." She said it with all the honesty that Peter's money afforded.

I understood. I got it. I don't doubt that Joely would not have fought for Nyla, except for the very concept that she explained. He couldn't afford to burn the bridge with Peter. Friend, bro, maybe out of necessity, loyalty, even love, but surely, mostly just as she explained. I could just see the mental personal ad of the slightly less advantaged: Wanted, one symbiotic relationship with a lonely tycoon.

For the second time today approaching the yacht voices could be overheard. Nyla gently tugged my shirt sleeve and motioned me to shh. We crouched down, her crouching and dragging me reluctantly along until we reached the open port hole.

"Joely, I support you in anything, but bro', this Topher deal. The 24-hour turnaround is never good Joely."

"Really Peter, cause you do it all the time. I hear you make deals like this every day and you come out shining like a new mint." I could hear the panic in Joely's voice rising, like teen angst right before the foot stomping, you can't tell me what to do.

Peter cool, calm, collective, "Exactly, I know from whence I speak. You, my friend, are the other guy in that scenario."

"Bullshit Peter. I guess this can't be shit since it didn't cross your desk first. Has it really come to this? If you can't take it, or create it, I can't make it. For real man, Pete, it's plenty of fish in the sea, bro."

"Precisely, but you my friend are fishing in a man-made pond, hand stocked. What details do you have? I mean, paperwork be damned. Joely, if you've learned nothing else in our professional relationship, come on man, you've got to know this isn't kosher. Fast money is exactly that: it goes just as quickly and unexpectedly as it comes. The manner you gain is the manner you lose."

We could hear Joely pacing back and forth across the wooden tiled floor.

"Listen Joely, give me the same 24 hours to look into this, if it's now or never…let it be never."

"Really Peter, you never brought me in on any deal. Never would be perfect timing for you. Heaven forbid I rise above my station, my father's station."

"Joely, be as ambitious as you want. I'm glad you sought your own deal. I don't bring you in on things because I know how important it is that you make it yourself. I can see why you want this. I know you don't want me to hand anything to you. I have you by my side so that you can learn and create something of your own. That belongs to you, from beginning to end. But this, this is not your starting line."

"Yeah Peter, it never is. I always got next. But if you take the best, then what value is next?"

The voices rose and fell in tempo, like a newly discovered concerto. But the waltz was unfamiliar, the tune unrehearsed. Nyla's hand covered her mouth, her eyes as large as the baubles around her neck. Theirs was an awkward dance, out of sync. The fear in her eyes told me that before the band played the final note; the waltz would become a fiery raging tango, and someone would be raked across the coals.

"You know Peter; you can control Nyla, even manipulate and interfere in Kary's life. But at some point other people's business involves just that other people. Not Peter! The point is, I see my position in your world Peter, not beside you; but beneath you, just like any other bitch in your life."

"Then don't go into this thing ass backwards!" We heard Peter's glass slam onto the desk. "Joely, this has simply gone far enough!" Peter's voice then simmered to calm.

Nyla squeezed my hand. The shivers that reverberated were not from the cool lake breeze, but the ice cold chill in Peter's voice. "Let me make it clear to you. Nothing, absolutely nothing in your life happens that is not orchestrated, manipulated or dictated; either by your actions or lack thereof. I pick up the pieces. I put them in play. I out maneuver. I out strategize. I deliver and you sign for the package every time. I am the goddamn details."

I motioned to Nyla that we needed to make a move one way or the other, she gently signaled to me to wait just another minute.

"My point is this, my and your anatomy and development is where the equality ends. My lineage, my wealth, my power, my presence and my legacy give me the privilege of ruler. And in the end, when we depart this earth, then and only then…"

Joely interrupting and speaking calmly for the first time since the altercation begin, "You do realize the monogram on the gates of that house will not be yours, don't you?" He even attempted snark with a side of raw emotion. "My point, my friend, is then you shall see equality."

I swallowed hard wondering just whom Peter would see as his equal. Vanity thou hath reached home base. The room still, the silence deafening. I crouched back around to the dock, dragging Nyla quietly along, she tugged back in resistance. The old awkward feeling started creeping in. This was way too much information. We heard the familiar sound of ice connecting with crystal and flowing liquid in a steady pour. Another round about to go down.

"Peter, I watched my dad lose everything to the Worthington life, and no disrespect, but I want different. I want a Joely Grant life. I have never been blind, but now I truly see. It appears you feel my progress is your regress."

Peter murmured over his glass, "Pgh, don't flatter yourself."

Frustrated Joely continued, "I'm not your man Geoffrey, I'm my own man. Peter, I just wanted to extend you an opportunity. Otherwise believe me, in hindsight I never would have said a word. I would have just collected and rode off into the sunset, until we meet again. It was just supposed to be a gesture of kindness, appreciation. A small investment for you, for me a gain of a lifetime."

Peter, who had remained silent, stated simply, "Walk away Joely".

"No Peter, whatever the outcome, I have to try."

"Joely, somewhere along the way Topher spotted your venerability. I don't know where, when or how, but you're a mark. Maybe it was in my absence, my preoccupation, I left you open."

"Damn Peter, man, it's not about you. This is about me for once. Just once, let it be me. Whatever it is, I'll pay the cost. What price freedom man?"

"Not nearly the cost of friendship."

"That's the point right there bro', friendship shouldn't cost nothing man."

"Yes, but one would pay dearly to keep it." We heard the soft tap of glass on fine oak, the sliding of a paneled door, and then absolute silence, broken by a single, er-hum.

Nyla let out an exhaustive breath and we walked hand in hand aboard home base. Nyla prepped herself with a quick run of the fingers through the hair, wiped her eyes and a fresh appliqué of cherry red Chanel.

"Lover, where you been hiding?" Peter winked as he crossed the room to embrace his wife. Nyla smiled and fell softly into his warm embrace, tilted her head back to look into his eyes and smiled warmly.

"Long day babe. Kary…" she averted her eyes when they fell on me. "Well, you know."

Peter, however, did not avert his eyes, but set them deadpan against me. "Something tells me Kary will be just fine." He followed with a smug expression, still in my direction. "She's resilient and infectious. Our little Kary will be just…fine."

I shuffled, hands in pocket, here we go with that awkward thing again. And again, I did not unlock from his gaze.

"Well" Nyla hugged Peter tightly and laid her head into his broad chest. Peter spoke "Good night, Abe."

"Yes Surr". I turned and walked away; as if one is allowed to turn his back to a God on earth.

I attempted once again the head back to the villa when I noticed Joely up on the pier, staring into the waters deep. The scowl on his face matched in perfect harmony the rising and falling of the choppy micro waves below. I took a deep breath, now was as good of a time as any. And well, Miss Scarlett, there may always be tomorrow but tomorrow may be too late. I waved as I quickened my pace onto the pier.

"Hey Man, just didn't want to pass without speaking." Joely gave a muffled grunt, still staring into the murky dark,

"Onto the pier is quite the pass."

"Semantics bro, along the way." I half chuckled.

Joely turned and gave me the ol' classic signature look of this crew. At least it wasn't the universal welcome sign, likely because both hands were in his pocket, probably in lethal balls of fists.

"Will this shut you up?" he handed me a well worn silver flask. I smiled and graciously accepted. I opened the lid and sniffed, not that it mattered, and took a long slow swallow.

"You can color me mum." I smiled, swigged again and leaned the flask his way. We swigged, savored and sulked in silence. The night and atmosphere so dark and heavy it almost made it seem as if the fog was the first to speak.

"Er-hum. Et tu, Brute?" Joely snarled out the words in my direction. "Get if off your chest man. Silence ain't your suite. I've had enough bullshit dumped on me tonight, what's one more pile." With that Joely lit a thin cigar, his Zippo held the flame in the wind. I pulled out my Marlboro. Joely passed the torch to me, a single rose etched into the dull silver. I caught the engraving on the back in the post lights of the pier, 'Every Rose Has its Thorn' hmmm. I spoke with caution as I handed the lighter back to him.

"Man, your friends are just concerned, you know. I mean, we all want one kind of peace or another. Like a strong wind behind us, the waves beneath us, all things that move us forward, keep us going. I'm not going to presume or speak on shit I know nothing about. But I do know I got a shifty vibe from Topher the moment I met him. I just, I mean, full disclosure, Nyla wanted me to talk to you. She's worried, and out of that worry she shared a little history.

Dude, I know where you are coming from. But I don't think this is the way to get where you want to be."

Joely shifted and his jaw clenched.

"Bro, I'm not trying to get in your business or piss you off. And I don't have an alternative solution, but I think you have friends that do."

"Mind your own fucking business Abe. This is my business and you have no fucking clue. You're just like them. You play back and forth because you don't have to choose. And you aren't stuck or fucked for that matter. You create fantasy in reality and you never have to know the difference."

Maybe I should have shut up, for whatever reason he turned his focus directly on me, and he really didn't know shit about my life. Fine, maybe it wasn't any of my business, but just as if he had decided to take a long walk off this short pier, I'd try to save him. He was taking a long shot on a short con, and I was trying to save him. But let him fight me, we both drown. I guess I kinda understood Peter right about now. Joely's thin frame was starting to sway, and it wasn't the wind. That was the only thing keeping its cool right about now. Joely's hands at his side started to curl in formation, and saliva gathered in the corners of his mouth.

I backed up, hands raised in surrender. "Dude, I can see I'm not helping. Last words, plain and simple advice; I don't trust Topher and neither should you. That's your reality, man."

"Fuck you Abe." He seethed. "You've done your bidding. Peter doesn't trust this deal because Peter doesn't believe anything exist that doesn't revolve around him and his world. Well this does exist, I do."

The shaking, the swaying and the spit bombs thoroughly accentuated his point, and I knew the pier on South Haven beach was not the place to push him over the edge. I once again assumed docile posture and turned to walk away. Joel continued to shout, enraged by circumstances, at my disappearing form.

"And you know what, I know stuff too. I didn't trust your shifty ass the first time I met you either." I paused and turned towards him. Maybe he was getting my point. I'd like to think we grew past the mistrust over the past few weeks. Maybe he was getting the difference between people who deserve a second a look and those you can see through. When you've seen enough and when you don't need to see anymore.

"I knew you weren't on the up and up, shady mother fucker." And then again, maybe not. I paused to give him audience, he deserved as much for his dramatic drunken rant. Okay, but I admit, I was getting a little pissed.

"Man, I thought you were some boy toy Kary brought along, seeking money, influence, a leg up. Couldn't be mad at that, watchful but not mad. But I never figured you for belonging here. But you my friend are not to be so trusted either. In vino veritas. And did Peter ever wine and dine on his little jaunt to Kalamazoo." He began walking towards me with a mix of shimmy and swagger. What exact elixir was in that flask? But I digress. Jokes aside this shit just got serious. I strolled forward and met him halfway. We reached the halfway mark, nose to nose.

"What. The. Fuck." My jaws clenched tighter as I strategically released each word from my vocal grasp. Joely snickered as he staggered back, and came forward with complete control.

"Alexander Barnabe Eyota." I felt my temple pulse, stopped dead where I stood. Joely began to cackle loudly weaving into a taunt, "My point precisely." The words slithered out of his mouth. Note this carefully, 'cause it will not happened again. I was shaken, rattled, and pissed the fuck off. But mostly I was found out. The lights flickered on the pier, and my cool shifted slightly to the left. Joely danced lightly away from the pier like Fred Astaire, singing in the rain, grooving through his pain.

Since my cool had only shifted slightly, I did not knock a fist sized hole in the fine oak paneled door when I reached the Captain's deck on home base. But the small soft glow inside told me I'd found my mark. Now I don't lose my cool completely, but...my blood was awfully warm. Before I could reconsider my fist sized renovations Peter opened the door and stared directly into me; his face stern, jaws tight and pure venom and malice in his eyes.

"Alexander Barnabe Eyota, Alexander the Great; clever, clever Abe." His mouth contoured into a sickening toothy glistening grimace; it revolted me to my core; but… not so much that I turned down the whiskey being offered.

"Peter, in all that I do, I am never intrusive. In all my observations I hold all truths I see. If you had something against me, or some concern, as a gentleman, and maybe that's where my truth failed me, you should have come to me first. It's called Respect, son."

"Respect my boy, is first and foremost earned; and earned essentially by truth, and son," he cocked his head in summation, "this in essence is where you failed yourself." Smooth as the backside of a Hersey bar, damn. Peter moved from the door and leaned against his captain's desk, packing his pipe as he held his gaze in my direction. I took a deep breath, the air bitter and riddled with, well truth.

"Peter, man, there is a reason why I go by my initials. It's complicated, but the reason is mine to own."

He gave a snarly smirk again, bit gently on his pipe. "Yeah, there is some reason alright, about a billion of them." For emphasis he strategically let out puffs on his pipe, 1, 2, 3, 4, pause 5. The man had done his homework.

I could feel the heat rising to my cheeks, and I felt that same clenched fist reasoning Joely resonated on the pier. Short walk, long drop. I gathered myself and spoke gently. "Of what possible benefit is this knowledge to you? My, my family, our wealth. You don't need us. You can't buy us. And there is nothing you can or will gain from us, from me."

"Essentially, you are correct my boy. I have no need for anything you own, possess, invest or digest."

Did he just "essentially" say what you eat don't make me shit? Damn, all phasers on stun.

"However, I told you when we met, I care for my friends, and their interests are my interests. And you and I, our mutual interests collide, I warned you to take care with that one mutual interest in particular."

I nodded in remembrance. "I never lied to Kary, and never would intentionally mislead or hurt her."

He blew out a smooth bourbon scent of Cavendish. "Omission my good man is the gateway to distrust."

I almost choked on the thick smoke, or maybe it was the irony. I conceded this one, it was way well played. I turned toward the door.

Peter lit his pipe, and being a gentleman, proceeded to walk me out. "Abe, I did look into you, and yes take this personal, but nothing has changed. Our friendship remains. As a man of means myself, I do have my reasons as well. Admittedly, not quite as many as you, but enough." He chuckled, I'm assuming in an attempt to lighten the mood. Not so much. "Abe, to some I'm a wolf, in couture, but a wolf none the less; touché. The disguise is all the better to see you with, etc, etc". He spread his palms in gesture and moved to shut the door.

Enough, way too funky to leave things unsaid. I cocked my head, hands behind my back in pensive thought, turned slightly with my parting retort; "Maybe instead of looking into your friends, your

time here would have been better spent looking after your friend."
The angry puffs matched my foot falls beat for beat.

I assume I made it back to my villa sans further interruption because
I woke up with a madgraine. I'm too skilled of a connoisseur to get a
hangover. No a madgraine is the direct result of having the vein in
your temple erupt multiple times in succession and your blood
pressure reach maximum mad as hell levels. Yeah, one of those
nights. I had lain down with the sunrise and awoken with the sunset.
I shuffled my way downstairs as the smell of fresh coffee two-
stepped its way upstairs.

Squeal, Squeak, Squawk, full capacity: seriously? "You're
up! I was worried about you. Coffee?" Again with the rapid
succession.

"Hair of the dog Kary, hair of the dog." I grumbled.

"I figured," she giggled. "So I prepared a Casablanca coffee
for you."

I etched a smile into my frown, errr? "Seagram's and
Sumatra," she snorted through her laugh.

I sipped and snickered. "Kary Parsons this could be the start of a beautiful friendship." We laughed in harmony, I refilled. And just like that we were back to us. She leaned down on the counter and grinned at me, a million dollars on the table…just like that.

We talked over coffee and cinnamon rolls. Kary actually baked, an old recipe from Nyla's grandma. Who knew these debutantes baked when stressed. That was uniquely cool and the rolls were uniquely delicious. I distinctly tasted bourbon and pecans.

"You're chipper this morning." I said between sips and bits.

"You were gone a long time and I had a long time to think." She pouted "You were out a lot yesterday."

I looked over my cup at her, "I tend to do that when expressly told to go away."

She punched me gently on the arm "Seriously, thank you. It gave me a lot of time to think and frankly be realistic about my future. I've decided I'm going to enjoy the next week and own up to all that is expected of me when I get home. Nyla and mom are right.

I have to start planning ahead. I'm expelled from the Garden Abe."
She scrunched her nose and wiggled her shoulders.

The black chiffon dress she wore added a certain maturity to her, if you don't count the peek-a-boo sheer skirt that revealed the dark briefs and toned thighs underneath. The dark and sheer contrast played against her shimmering skin. One of the straps slipped, and revealed the sleekness of her shoulder and high curve of her chest, caught by the last light of the setting sun. It was like the lightly toasted pastry in front of me. I imagined all she encompassed; her sweetness, sugar and spice, her intoxicating laughter and her nuttiness that drove me completely out of my mind. I bit into another roll as she smiled, and uttered softly under my breath, "Delicious."

"Okay, let's play truth or dare" she giggled.

"Nah, Nah, if you want to tell me something just say it. I'm not playing your little game."

"Oh come on Abe, what are you afraid of, a little truth."

I hid behind my cup, a little. Was this her way of getting me to confess? Had Peter said something to her? I wasn't playing, and I wasn't saying, at least not this way.

"Come on Abe, okay I truth, you gotta dare."

"Okay. Fair is fair. So truth Kary Parsons."

"Okay" She took a deep breath. "Mama made it clear to me that with daddy's advanced age, income won't regenerate forever, and while now our money works for us, it does still require some sort of overseeing, for lack of a better term, a skill neither mama nor I possess in abundance. And long story short Ma' has no intention of compromising her lifestyle to accommodate either of our shortcomings. Mama's nothing if she's not beautiful and brutally honest. Daddy calls it feisty, I have other choice words. Anyway, I well, I may have to succumb to a suitor when I get back, Buford Klaus Remington the III, to be precise. So no more Eden Club, and no more of this." She jutted her chin forward in a high road manner, and let the statement stand.

I heard no more of us and felt a slight palpitation. But then again, she said it with such resolve and all matter of fact; completely drama free, which is completely not Kary Parsons, that I guess neither of us took it as a "truth"…at the time. So I, with determinedly matching resolve said, "Kary, we will always have this. We're friends, and our friendship will get us through anything. Besides, how bad can Buford Klaus Remington the Third really be?" We both erupted in laughter. We know the type.

"Okay" she leaned in close and in one hot breath whispered "Dare". Casablanca was in full effect.

"Okay, okay. Give it your best shot."

"I will." Her eyes danced as she contemplated my impending dare. At the mere mention of shot, and not one to let irony and opportunity pass I got out the Cuervo. A few shots later she was ready. "Abe, your dare is to run out and do a lap around the pool, Full Monty!"

"Errr, in the pool? Don't you know you shouldn't swim for up to thirty minutes after you eat?"

"First of all, contrary to your popular belief, alcohol is not a meal, and secondly I mean run around. No hiding in the water."

"I don't know, despite your coffee, it ain't exactly Moroccan sunshine out there."

She shouted, "Abe, fair is fair!!!"

"Ah, my words find their way back to me. Okay, but watch it now, you might see something the likes of which you ain't never seen before, I'm taking the dare, but don't be scared of the magnitude of the truth it holds!"

"Whatever!" she giggled and chased me out to the patio. We reached the private area with low well-landscaped bushes for neighbors. I turned my back to her and went Full Monty, her words; mine, buck naked; and made a mad dash around the pool. We laughed hysterically but as I round to first head on, the rose flush in her cheeks told me she definitely saw something the likes of which she had never seen. The glint in her eyes told me if I challenged her on the truth, well, the grin on her face told me she'd likely be up to the challenge, and probably dare me to try again. I promised myself that million dollars was worth the work. I dressed and we headed back inside.

She turned to me "I needed that laugh."

"Oh, so I'm a big joke to you huh."

She winked, "Well, you're no joke," followed with a mischievous grin.

"But one last truth, how did you know about Buford?"

"I have my ways. But thank you for telling me. I know it's not a game. I've had a bit of reality shoved down my throat in the past day or so too." I reached out and held her hand.

She gently let her hand slide to her side and started to fiddle with the napkins on the counter. "Abe," She looked questioningly up at me, "Honestly, I thought you would have more of a reaction to the whole Buford situation, I mean all kidding aside. I just…" She shrugged her left shoulder, biting gently on her inner lower lip.

I interrupted, it was a statement that she couldn't finish and I couldn't begin. "Don't over think it, Kary. It's probably just the nerves and highs and lows of the past few weeks and close quarters is way more than we expected. All the decadence and indulgence and realizing somewhere it's got to end, and figuring out back to normal; what that really means. If you weren't serious or worried about Buford before, why worry about him now? Like I said, I think all this is coming up because of where we are; you're back with your old crew with all the same expectations. We both kind of carved out our own individual existences back home, with just enough to keep our minds off of how it really all comes to be. Cornerstone is doing its job: reminding us of where we want to be, who we are and where we belong. Like it or not, we each have to determine our status quo. I'd like to be part of yours and have you part of mine, but I wouldn't dare add or subtract to that without giving you a chance to decide the baseline for your happiness." I gently nudged her cheek, "And that's enough, you're the one that chose a truth." I kissed her softly on the cheek through grinning lips.

Her eyes welled with tears. I thought she was going for a tissue, but she picked up the late edition of the New York Times, and right there, Page 6, front and center, Buford Klaus Remington III, breaking ground on their newest department store. The checkered

jacket and high water pants were enough, but the receding hairline

surely put things over the top, more or less. In hindsight it may have

been poor timing, but at the time I admit, I broke down in pure,

unapologetic, hysterical laughter. When I looked up from my all

fours, floor slapping position, Kary was trembling with laughter too.

Thank God. Gotta hand it to the girl, crying through her pain. Yes,

Kary Parsons, our friendship will get us through anything. This will

always be enough; but The-us (thus), how far can it take my heart.

Upon recovery I went up to shower. Kary was supposed to meet the

girls for early cocktails. She invited me to join when I was done.

"Abe, I'm out." I heard her shout as the door closed. One of

the rare and few times I did not want to be synonymous with liquor.

All I could do was pray my name did not come up during drinks, but

it was Kary Parsons, so how unlikely was that.

It had started to drizzle by the time I got out of the shower. My madgraine was long gone and warm happy thoughts filled me once again. Dramatic I know, but bliss or blitzed getting over being pissed is all good, anytime. I thought I'd try Kary's new drink theory and experimented with a whiskey martini, pitcher sized of course, sticking with the proper way to do things. I needed music, but wasn't quite in the mood for the Shakely, funk your mind sound. So I settled on the unconventional around here, classical music station; *heavens to murgatroid*. He turned it to AM.

I had called the concierge to start a fire prior to my shower. So by now the room was warm and toasty. I pulled back the sliding door to the patio so I could catch true classical music, the sound of natural rainfall, during station breaks. The light evening brought music into my heart. The radio and atmosphere brought it to my soul as I sipped and dozed, dozed and sipped, and grooved all up and through. It was almost home. I was jolted awake by the click of the lock and the fumbling of the door knob. I didn't think it was locked, and wasn't going to disrupt my cozy by getting up. But I did turn the radio down and listened with tipsy eagle eyes. That's the level of

tipsy you've got to just understand.

I then heard sobs. My heart leaped and sunk and leapt again. What

the hell? I raced to the door carefully navigating Prada, Halston and

Westwood. I opened the door to a sobbing, soaking wet Kary. Under

any other circumstances, well, you can imagine the level of detail,

but this wasn't that type of occasion. The only thing stirred at the

sight of her drenched in the doorway were my emotions. Who, what,

when, where, all followed by "in the hell", fuck the how and why.

Two things you do not do in my book, fuck up my buzz and make

my Kary cry. The fan better look out cause something's coming its

way.

Enough! I pulled her gently from the doorway and into my

arms, and kicked the door closed. I held onto her long enough to stop

the trembles. Then reached for the towel I had left strewn on the

banister, and dried her hair. I patted dry the rest of her as

unobtrusively and gently as possible. I poured her a small sifter of

brandy and placed an assortment of pastries, cheeses and fruit slices

in front of her. Mom always said comfort food wouldn't have its own category if it wasn't meant to be eaten during times of stress and strife. With this in mind, I called the delivery service and ask them to send a selection of pastas and sauces over with an array of bread and rolls.

I proceeded gently with her. "Kary, tell me what's happened." Momentarily, I selfishly wondered if she found out about my family, if she was hurt by my perceived deception. But knowing Kary as I do, news like that would likely result in a punch, a series of squeaks, squeals and squawks; or more punches.

"Kary, honey, you've got to talk to me." I knelt in front of her and held her hands.

She sniffled, and spoke. "It's Nyla." Her breath quickened and before she could break down completely I grasped her hands tighter, leaned closer.

"I'm here, take your time. Let me help you." I kissed her gently on the forehead, freshening her brandy. As she drank, she calmed enough to speak.

"I guess dumbass Joely took some dumbass deal with shifty ass Topher. Nyla heard him on the phone with his banker confirming basically everything he has is going into the damn deal. Nyla called Peter from their bedroom and went down to stop Joely. Well, that's what Peter heard. I don't know if they struggled, or if she slipped on the deck, with the rain and all, but, but Nyla..." I couldn't help the breath that I sucked in from shock, as I too myself begin to tremble, anticipating the worst in her next words.

I forced myself to calm. "Nyla's what, sweetheart?" If it was truly the worst she had to find the words herself, the reality had to come from within in order for her to process, to grieve.

"No, no..." she breathed in and out a calming breath. I leaned in and raised her head to meet my eyes. "No." I shook my head in time with hers. "No, I mean, she's, thank God, she's not that. She is banged up pretty bad, some sprains or something, a concussion I think, but she. I still have my best friend, my sister." With that she collapsed in my arms and cried to her heart's content. After about a half hour, she spoke softly and quietly, but much more at ease. I listened and held onto her, my best friend.

"It's just, Peter found her, you know. Just laying there, just laying there. And Joely, those bastards were halfway across the lake, oblivious. Had to be, right?" She looked up at me.

"Right." I said with every confidence in Joely. He would never leave Nyla. No end to that statement, not ever.

She smiled with our faces just inches apart, she softly whispered, "Abe, Abe, I love you."

I kissed her lightly on the lips, "I know" and held her as close and tight in my arms as she felt in my heart. I knew in that moment that this was, she was, enough. But as moments go, the doorbell startled us back into our villa in South Haven, back from whereever it is our souls had journeyed. The thing about enough is sometimes you only recognize it in hindsight.

The food was delivered. As I set up, Jai came barging through the closing door. Looking I might add like hell on heels. "I could kill that motherfucker with my bare hands. Son of a bitch, piece of shit, lowdown bastard. Ass!"

Jai was never one not to tell us how she really feels. "I could rip out his fucking juggler and feed it back to him inside out."

Damn. She stormed into the middle or the room and in that moment we locked eyes. If she could cry, if she cried, I think in that moment she would have sobbed like a baby.

"Jai, any news?" Kary jumped up hastily, dropping the blanket I had managed to cover her with earlier. She wobbled dizzily to the counter and leaned against it for support.

"Yea, this just in, you need to eat. And I need a – Oh, thanks Abe." I handed her a brandy and Kary another small one. Jai continued with the real update. "Well, Nyla's going to be okay, so Abe you can hold off on replacing her creepy on the spot with a drink before you askedness." That brought air-lifting light chuckles, a welcome relief and release for us all. "She should be home within the hour."

"Oh jeez," Kary slowly getting back to herself. "Someone's got to tell Madeline." She sat her plate down and started looking around for shoes and umbrella.

"Whoa, whoa, not you my dear, you sit, eat!" Jai gave her an insistent touch back into her chair.

Mortimer had just walked in and overheard, "Hey, I'm fresh from the rain, let me go, you guys stay dry. We don't need anybody catching cold."

I shook my head in protest, "Jeez, you sound like a grandma, but you make a good point. So take your own advice. Stay. Dry off – towels upstairs. Have some brandy, or grab something from the bar and eat. We ordered plenty. I slept all day and relaxed so let me take the load." I thought old friends could help cheer Kary up a little faster, or be there if she broke down completely. Give her a chance to take off the brave face she tried to keep up for me. Also keeping both of us from doing something we may not be ready for. Grief, shock, fear, anger, pain – make strange bedfellows dontcha' know.

Mortimer chimed in, "But for real, maybe I should go in case Topher's ass shows up."

"In that case maybe I should go, or go too." Jai shook out her drying fedora from the banister, placed it low on her head and crossed her arms.

"In either case, I think I better do this alone. If Topher is there, it may just result in a single ass whooping as opposed to a total annihilation."

Jai and Mortimer both said in unison "Careful with the skilled fighter angle."

I retorted, "Hey, we just don't need to go all Super Friends on his ass just yet."

The comment elicited the second round of laughter for the night. A crew that keeps each other lifted; now I could sail off into the sunset with cats like that.

As I headed out I realized I hadn't grabbed a jacket, and the rain was starting to pick up. I ducked back around and into the carport connected to our villa, deciding the weather warranted using the scooter. Besides Madeline was one of the "far-enders". Five minutes later I was pulling into the far end. I noticed their Gold Cart wasn't pulled into the port all the way so I backed up and parked out front. I headed up the gated cobblestone walk way. I didn't see any lights on in the front window, so I figured I'd peek around the back before knocking. If Madeline was resting because she had heard the news or had a headache or anything I didn't want to be the one to disrupt her rest.

From what I could already see in the side windows, the far end was far out. Crystal chandeliers, antique furnishings, and gold finishes. I thought our bar was top shelf. But even from this view I could tell one of the shelves read like a history book. I mean the dates went way back. Cutting my time warp short, I proceeded to the back patio area for signs of life. I saw Madeline standing on the patio in a red very mini harem dress with loose cutout straps for sleeves. The top, cropped in back, defied the laws of physics and held her full bosom front side, exposing a cleavage spilling v-neck, connected with crystal and gold chain to a silky thin fabric and sheer chiffon bottom. It was well above her thighs, or more accurately just beneath her ass, that made the dress in its entirety, all completely barely there. She stood barefoot on the patio and pulsing through my veins.

I was about to announce myself when I heard a deep baritone bellowing across the patio and moving closer. Shocked back into reality, I realized Topher was here. I wondered what happened with him and Joely. Did they know? Did he, or Madeline know about Nyla? Where was Joely anyway? So I did the Abe thing and scrunched down for a good listen. I'd worry about apologies and forgiveness if I got caught. I silenced my mind as I caught wind of the nature of the conversation.

"But Tops, none of that matters, just give them the money back and say how you saw that it was a bad deal. You'll look like a hero, be a hero." Madeline pleaded.

"That shit looks shady Madeline, shady as fuck. That ain't my bag anyway. It ain't how it goes down in the streets of the real world."

"Streets, really Topher. When were you last 'in the streets'? Where is this even coming from? You've never acted, you've never been…" she paused, "this. I thought, I mean."

"Look ma', this shit is real. What you thought I was like you? Not even close. When opportunity knocks sweetheart..."

"You abandon all" Madeline sniffled.

"Will you shut the fuck up?!" Topher paced, sweat glistening on his forehead, and saturating his pale shirt. "This shit is not a joke. Oh Tops it's just a few million, just give it back. Are you that fucking daft? Give it back? This is my shit, my time. You thought I was just going to sit on the sidelines, being part of your life? Man please, I gots to get my own. I don't need shit that's ours 'cause you say it ours. I need mines, and I know it's mine. You ain't deep enough to understand where I'm coming from and I sure as hell don't need you and no hoity-toity where I'm going. Hustling everyday to keep up, to stay in, that's not enough. Living off of ain't living Madeline."

"Ah, the convenient truth, now it's not enough. Now you're living off of me. Funny how I thought we were building something together. I'm neither blind nor daft Topher. I was in love. What you consider living off me, I saw as having your back, supporting your dreams." Madeline's voice shook, but she was holding her own admirably, considering the circumstances.

"Wake up! Hello! It was all a dream. But this, this right here, this money, smell that, a scent stronger than smelling salt. I'm woke and walking now. Walking away from people who look at Versailles and call it a tacky shit house, people who own their friends, all the spoon feeding and hand holding. Your damn friends walking up in here like they own my shit too. Fuck all ya'll motherfuckers. Whoo!" He was drunk on his perceived power and it was earth shattering to hear. A few aluminum cases to seal his fate and break her heart; Jai's juggler plan was sounding like an applicable enterprise.

"Tops, I understand. I understand the freedom. Let's just start over, do this with your truth. Let me give the money back, and call it even. You keep yours, and I, I keep you. Even Steven, okay."

"That statement alone proves, you don't understand at all. Let me give you a clue. It's not me, it's you. I don't want to do this anymore. You're right about one thing, the freedom. It's going to be a beautiful thing Madeline, for both of us, finally. Enjoy it doll, enjoy it."

"Topher, if you are serious, I can't let you do this to my friends. I feel responsible. I brought you into their lives. I trusted you and out of respect for me they did the same. Topher, somebody worked for all the things we have. Somebody worked for the things you are taking away."

"That's just it. Somebody, you've had shit so long you don't even know who or how you got it. It just is, always was."

"Tops, you know that is untrue. I've earned a lot of what I have."

"But it has to have a jump off point, and a cushion if you fall, a home base, if you will. Now I've got mine. Be done, Madeline. I am."

"Done Topher? When were we done?" She asked weakly.

I could have answered for him. Instead, I listened patiently for the expected.

The reply, cold as the steel cases holding his future, "Before we ever began." A noise around the front turned our attention. Madeline turned to look, as did I. When our gazes returned to the patio, Topher was ghost.

My first thought was to follow suite. Then I remembered the scooter out front, fi-uck. I saw a light shine through the gates. Damn, he was taking my scooter. I decided the best alternative was to go in like I should have done in the first place. But after the conversation I had overhead, I wasn't sure if even I was capable of finding the right words to say. I took a deep breath and jogged around to the front, another deep breath and knocked on the door. Madeline opened the door and just stared at me. I leaned against the archway and smiled.

"Don't you have this scene backwards, shouldn't I be the one standing in the doorway it a tight, sopping wet shirt, looking all sexy, woebegone and wanton." She said as a slow seductive smile crept across a face. For a girl that just got her heart broken, she was a nice piece of work. For the record she was a nice piece of work on any given day, under anybody's circumstance.

"Suit yourself." I pulled her towards me and swung her around until she was in the door, mildly moist and looking sexy, woebegone and wanton as hell. She cracked up and pushed me back inside with her lips and hips. As I was willfully backed into the room, her back leg gave the door the old heave hoe. I wish I could say I behaved like a gentleman and broke the enchanting, all encompassing full body kiss, but…I grabbed her soft curls and held on. I'm nothing if not honest. I didn't let go until a full five seconds after she did.

"Uh, Madeline, I'm…" I struggled with an apology.

"Shh," she put a finger to my lips. "Don't ruin it." She licked her lips, top and bottom, kissed me again, then gently pulled away. My lips still held her taste, top and bottom. She handed me a drink I didn't even notice her fixing. Yeah, her kiss was that intoxicating. As I drank she slipped her hand down her curvaceous form and tickled playfully between fabric and chiffon, brought it slowly up to my glass and ran a slow moist finger around the rim. She sipped from my cup and pushed in toward my mouth. I traced the rim and emptied the glass like one would a shot. The flavor may have been bourbon but the taste was all Madeline, bottom to top. This must be what the Gods mean by nectar.

The phone rang softly in the distance. She shook her head indicating her plan to ignore it, but it did remind me of my original intent. I guess my distraction is a viable enough excuse, but not really. I pulled back giving some distance between us, our bodies. Focus.

"Madeline, do you know about Nyla? The girls sent me over to tell you."

"I heard," She hesitated, sipped from her own drink and relaxed her shoulders, "from Topher. I guess him and Joely heard the emergency call on the boat and raced back to shore. Topher dropped Joely off somewhere, went to handle their business and showed up here about a half an hour ago. I couldn't face the girls Abe. I just couldn't." She paused to breathe and blurted out "Topher's gone, Abe. He betrayed me, my friends, and now he's just gone. I can't let him get away with what he's done. He's going to tell Joely the deal was a bust. A bad investment, and walk away with his and a few other people's money. It's bad, Abe. I don't know if I should talk to

Peter or what I should do. But you can't treat people like this, not people who love you."

"Madeline, it would require that he felt the same at some point. From what I can gather, he did not."

"Maybe I always knew that, but…it was close enough."

"Not once you know the real thing sweetheart." I rubbed her arms and held her hands.

"I know the real thing, it hurts and heals way more. So this, this will pass because it was only close enough."

"Trust the process." I raised my glass.

"Trust the process." She toasted in return. "He's not coming back is he? Topher's not coming back." I think the finality of it all was beginning to set in.

"I know honey, I know." I hugged her and she embraced me tightly as her body shook like thunder and the tears fell like rain. We sat there on the floor until the phone broke the silence, only to stop ringing abruptly.

"That reminds me; I should call the girls and let them know I'm here and what not." I rose to dial the villa.

"Abe" Madeline called after me, "Please, do me a favor. Don't mention Topher and all that. I will have to find a way to deal with him, to deal with Peter. Tomorrow."

I nodded acknowledgement. Thankfully Jai answered the phone. I told her I was with Madeline. She asked me to tell her Nyla was home from the hospital, resting at the villa. Hopefully we could look in on her later. Kary was resting as well. She paused on the latter. "Mortimer and I are going to stay here with Kary, just be together for now. So, see you soon?" Question. Some air time.

"See ya." Statement. As I replaced the receiver, Chanel No 5 wafted its way through my nostrils and I turned around right into glitter, sparkles, Boudreaux glistening lips, and thick curled sensual chocolate.

"You want to go to Oz, Dorothy?" Deep throaty whiskey-filled breath and a slow hand engulfed me and my very personal space. Madeline slide down, way past Kansas, the tornado picked up speed and siphoned everything in its path. In the next moments, I daren't click my heels at all.

Madeline re-applied her lipstick and perfume, I caught my breath. She served up two shots of history from the top shelf and smiled, "Emerald City, deary?"

"Take me to the Wizard damn it." I slammed my glass on the counter.

"Wherever the road takes us." She winked at me over her shoulder.

"Where you lead I follow." We laughed and skipped arm in arm down the cobblestone path all the way to the waiting Limo.

Emerald City was what one can only describe as like, the Arkham [Asylum] bookmobile. It was a juke joint on wheels, seeming to appear only after the moon has taken its place in the dark night sky and dusk is long gone. So this is where 'the people' jived. From the rib-flavored air, which was that thick, to the strong, eye-burning grade of liquor, right down to the fragrant herb which I can only deduce puts the green in Emerald City; this place was outta' sight.

After a few moments of indulgence, Madeline led me to the long bar, waved a whisky my way. My eyes followed her to the dance floor. She was immediately engulfed by a swarm of pinstripes, drooping suspenders and white cotton undershirts, flying skirts, and lots of barely there. I felt a phrase coming on, 'this joint is jumpin'. I grinned as I watched her move like a queen among them. Like sweet amber, she swirled and glistened in the thick hot smoky air. It was raw. It was tribal. It was truth. It was freedom, and I thank God in this moment, I am alive. When there was a break in the swarm, the sweet honey sweat dripping from the bodies of the beautiful people like sap from a strong maple, she motioned me to join. But I didn't want to ruin the view by smoking the hive. So I watched. The rippled muscles, the taunt bodies, the full hips and low dips. The writhing and wiggling of the deep brown sea ebbed and flowed like the most natural and majestic of all God's creations, life giving water and man and woman. As the band played on, the refrain of the final song, I find replaying in my mind at times and I just revel in the moment with a smile.

The strong drinks, the herbal incentive, and intoxicating atmosphere started to merge into a gyroscope of motion. Certainly before dawn rose, I was lost in barely there ruby red. My pulse quickened. The high swinging lights rocked into slow methodic movement: a thrusting, grinding, dance of creation, swimming in life giving waters, devouring nectar's source. Bodies absorbing the essence of being, as sheer and chiffon gave way to leather, leather gave way to marble, and marble to Egyptian cotton, and alas cotton to skin: the beginning of all things and endings that will stain our memories for time eternal. For in this is the truth I seek. For in this is the answer I shall find. For to this succumbs enough.

The last melodic sound I heard, before a final quivering burst, was the slight clicking of a door.

The rough beach sand, along with the shrieking in my ear, made me curse the heels that clicked and ended night. This wasn't Kansas and it sure as hell weren't home.

"Abe, wake the fuck up. Topher's gone. Shit's all fucked up. Get up." Jai was standing over me, rousing me awake. I woke up, sand stuck all in the unknown; drenched in sweat, and well, let's just leave it at sweat. What the fuck?

I tried to get oriented as Jai continued. "Where were you? We called Madeline's but she said you left to take a walk. I find you here. Joely's all out of sorts, and Peter's so cool he's calm. Abe, you better clean yourself up and get presentable. By the way Mortimer brought the scooter back from Madeline's for you."

"Thank him, please. I've got to get to the villa. Is Kary alright?" I was still shaking out the cobwebs but quickly coming up to speed.

"You've got bigger problems, Peter wants to see you."

"Aw jeez, the Lord beckons. Jai, I'm not in the mood for his shit."

"I think it's worth wading through this time though," she smiled. "If nothing else, than to be done. They are leaving soon. Nyla needs to recuperate somewhere else."

I got to my feet, "Well, since you put it that way." I shuffled off to the villa to 'make myself presentable'. Came to in the shower. Washed, dried, and did my best to bring my funky back. I called out to Kary, no response. That bothered me, but something else was bugging me too, something I missed. Uncharacteristic of me really, my observation skills are usually top notch.

I headed down for coffee. This morning, this and only this morning, I drank my coffee black and straight. I had a feeling today was going to call for a change of pace. I figured Kary might be visiting Nyla at her far end villa so I decided to head there first. I hadn't seen Nyla since the accident either. I wanted to check in on her as well. Although I was feeling much better, my legs were still on a rhythmic beat all their own, so I took the scooter. Surprisingly

Nyla was not at the villa. No one was. As a matter of fact it was shut up tight. I turned around and pointed the scooter in the direction of home base; back to where it all begin.

I reached home base, parked the scooter and climbed aboard. "Knock, Knock."

"Abe!" Nyla limped slowly towards me.

"Hi sweetheart, how are you." I hugged her carefully. The fresh bruises on her face had barely started to heal. I noticed a cast on her arm.

She caught my glance. "Like my crystal armor? Peter had it customized to suit."

"Thoughtful guy."

She smiled weakly. "A drink?"

"No, I'm alright. Let me make you something though."

"Well, with the pain meds, I better not. Maybe you could just hit blend on that daiquiri concoction there though." We laughed in unison. You have to admire a woman who springs back so quickly. I poured us each a glass and settled into one of the plush seats by the bar.

"You doing okay for real?"

She bit her lip slightly, hesitated before speaking, and exhaled a slow breath, "I will be." She sat on the seat next to me and I could see the tears welling in her eyes. "Abe, I was so hurt. Everything just came to a head out of nowhere. Why now? How could Topher do something like this? You know I haven't even seen Madeline in the past couple days, she has got to be mortified. And Joely, all these years, what is it that makes people who've waited take that chance, wrong or right? It's like they reach a breaking point that never really had a set level. Maybe one could argue that when the opportunity presents itself, that's when you find your breaking point. I don't know. I mean couldn't you just work harder to make opportunities for yourself? People do that all the time, don't they?"

"Some people are now or never. Maybe these two just reached their now at the same point in time. Or maybe Topher is just an asshole and Joely was just desperate. I can't answer for him. But I am certain whatever it was, Topher saw it and pounced."

She looked down into her glass.

"Trust me, the answer's not in the bottom, I look all the time." That got a smile from her.

"Abe, I hated him. For just a brief moment I really hated him."

"Topher?" She shook her head.

"Joely?" Again, no.

"Peter," she whispered "Peter. In the hospital, slipping in and out of consciousness, I heard him before he came into my room. He was so cocky about how right he was, about how Joely shouldn't try to go around him. How he didn't know how Joely ever thought that he could amass a fortune or even fortune starter through the likes of Topher. And me, I felt like an afterthought, or even worse still, a prize. But damn it Abe, I chose him just as much as he chose me.

Abe, how can two people be so different? How can love be love, but so different in each heart"

"You and he?" I asked.

She went on. "It wasn't love that brought me back, it was hate." She rose from our seats and moved behind the bar. She knelt down as she talked. Since her voice was fading, I rose and leaned over the bar to hear and continue the conversation. She hit a button hidden somewhere behind the bar and it slid towards me. I jumped back, startled by a movement that stopped no sooner than it had begun. She moved a tile that was beneath the bar to reveal a combination safe.

"This yacht was my father's. Peter doesn't even know this is here." She gave a sinister little giggle from deep within her throat. She turned the dial, 12, and continued to speak. "You know Abe, hate can build things too. Hate is roses." 24. "It feeds off the dirt from the ground, the heat of the sun, the drenching water, something beautiful emerges, but with thorns that can pierce and tear, make blood or love depending on how one handles it." 36. She poured the remainder of an open bottle of Seagram's hundred-proof gin into her strawberry daiquiri. Tears flowed from her eyes as she swallowed down the spiked red slush. A little trickled from the corners of her mouth, like remains of a fresh kill in the cheeks of a lioness.

"Nyla Rose. Maybe that is what my mother meant in the name, Abe. Watch out for the thorns! Tonight, I almost pricked him Abe." 7. "I almost turned his Heaven into Olympus, where more than one God exists. I alone have that power. But he saved himself, because that what Peter does, he saves himself." She tugged on the door and a soft wisp revealed the contents to her. She took the papers out and held them in her hands, her lips twisted into a sinister looking half pout, half smile; and flattened out into an even line. Tears slowly dripped from her chin onto the dried parchment envelopes. She dabbed the fragile paper softly with her palm and returned the documents to the dark abyss deep in belly of the yacht. The precious power safe from Peter's grasp. Ever a media mogul's daughter, she slammed the door shut, gave the dial a spin, and replaced the tile safely back in alignment with the others. She hit the button to slide the bar back into its proper place and leaned against the wall, exhausted from the effort and emotional expenditure. She begin to mumble and slide slowly down the wall, "My Peter, my love, who saves himself – and handler of all the flowers in his garden with the greatest of care: even those who began as he."

I reflected in silence; Nyla's ultimate power, Peter's empire and financial security, a delicate balance, and true love in their manmade heaven. I kneeled down beside her, tucked her loose hairs behind each ear and kissed her lightly on the forehead. "Goodbye Nyla Rose."

As I stepped from the yacht I saw Peter and Joely in deep conversation. Peter looked in my direction so I waved. He beckoned me over.

"Abe, I must confess. You were right, I didn't protect my friend. I am confident and man enough to admit my error. I couldn't see his ambition, his need for something beyond my provision. Alas too, your secret is safe with me. In light of it all, and looking at Joely's motivation, I see why you choose to keep love and money as distant relatives. It works for you. It may yet work for Joely with a woman that believes she has a choice. I think, however things work out with Kary and yourself, it won't be the result of my interference."

I didn't believe him for a second. But he believed it in the moment, so that was most likely going to end up on the books as truth.

"Now my good man, I truly wish you luck and happiness, because you sure as shit don't need the money." He slapped me on the arm and we shared a laugh. Why not? That could definitely go on the books as truth. Every now and then you gotta just own what is. Joely smiled and headed to prepare his boat for departure.

"Peter" I caught his arm before he turned back to the yacht. "What about..?" I nodded my head in Joely's direction.

Peter turned slightly to follow my eyes and returned his gaze to me, and parted his lips in a slow grin. "Forgive, but not forget. If you forget you lose your breadth and tool for measure; measurement of change, positive or negative, better or worse."

I interrupted, "Richer or Poorer."

He looked me dead in the eye, "I don't even understand the concept." With that he tipped his hat, leaning it slightly to the side, shook my hand and we parted as friends.

I watched as they sailed off with plans to eventually dock on the French Riviera so Nyla could heal and tan and try Platinum Blondedom. As Home Base sailed away, a smaller sleeker boat followed behind.

I no longer wonder who the little lamb was, and who was sure to follow.

I thought about going by Madeline's to see how she was doing. I didn't expect anything after last night but I did want to make sure that we were cool. I thought better of it though, with the whole Topher situation. She may want time to process the whole ordeal. The last thing she needed was me popping up on her doorstep. Maybe she regretted last night. Maybe she didn't want to over think it. Maybe I shouldn't either. I stood on the beach alone and watched the storm clouds roll away as the sun fought for its rightful dominion over the afternoon sky.

I figured it was time to leave Cornerstone and head out to parts a little less grounded in too much. I stopped at the Welcome Center to make a couple of calls for transportation. There were some costly last-minute travel arrangements including begs, pleads, and you-owe-me's, but mission accomplished.

I also took the time to rearrange and prioritize things in my mind, mainly Kary Parsons with her goofy, flighty, dramatic, beautiful self. She ran the gamut of my emotions. I knew, as a writer with a few good stories in me, a gamut of emotions was good – very good. I knew that when something or someone keeps popping up or catching you by surprise, you keep seeking: Like my attraction to Madeline, like my indulgence and fondness for this group of people that a few weeks ago I would have, from the other end of the bar, ordered another round for one, on. Like the very thing that brought me here, like the because of it all. That missing bit that drew me in, always has me, and that draws me back when I start to stray or stumble too far off course. That piece of me that knows with reason now, what I only thought I knew before entering this milieu: Yes, Kary Parsons: I. Want. In.

As I walked towards the villa, I let the last few thoughts of Cornerstone float gently out to sea. Reflected on the past few weeks: the crew, the things I'd observed and absorbed about friendship, ambition, truth, love…myself. Then I did the next logical thing…I followed my heart.

I arrived back at the villa to find Kary all packed up and ready to go.

"We're heading out?" I said, a little shocked that she hadn't mentioned nor noted a departure date up to now; and even more so that she was going to just leave, leave me.

"No. I don't know. I'm leaving. There is really no reason stay. The week's almost over. I'm not going to be writing and doing these little gigs anymore. Quite honestly I'm Cornerstone'd out." She fiddled with her bags and purse, avoiding all eye contact with me.

"Kary, seriously, were you going to leave without telling me? That's a little cold blooded for you. I, I didn't… Did I piss you off somehow?" I felt like I was being kicked in the stomach repeatedly. A tad nauseous, I felt a cold sweat coming on. I don't know what I could have done to make her just walk away. We always find a way to talk things out. When I left last night, her leaving seemed to be the farthest thing from her mind. Her leaving me never even crossed mine.

She turned to me with a half smile, "It's just time for me to go, to face reality. Real life Abe, not Eden Club, not Cornerstone, not anything crafted, constructed, built or based on fantasy. I'll see you around back home, Abe. I'll take care of any of your travel stuff. I dragged you here, the least I can do is get you out. Leave whenever you want, with whoever you want." She motioned to the porter the last of her bags were ready and started to gather the remainder of her carry on items.

I rushed towards her and grabbed both her hands firmly. "What are you doing? Just give me a minute," I pleaded.

"To say goodbye," She snarked.

"What? No, just to explain or something."

"Explain what Abe, you've clearly decided where you wanted to be last night. And now, this morning, Madeline won't even answer the phone. Go be where your heart wants to be, I have a life waiting for me."

"Madeline, what are you talking about that, that..." I paused searching for the right words, searching for the truth, to tell her like it was, like it is, like I mean it. "You know what Kary Parsons you're right. Last night I did figure out where I want to be. I saw the core of everything I wanted and needed. I went to walk on the beach, to make it go away, to think it out and apparently to sleep it off. All I did was set it in stone. When I woke up Madeline was on my mind. But all the thoughts that ran through me didn't go away. They were made clear."

She tried to pull away from me, "Abe, really I don't need to hear this shit. There is no way in hell you don't see how I feel about you. You even said it last night. You know. What you're doing now, I don't need an explanation. I get it. Madeline is everything I'm not and never will be. I'd list it all, but you know that too, and quite frankly it's a long depressing list."

We both smiled.

"Anyway, this has been one of the most exhausting times of my life. I just want to go home! I'm glad the hero gets the girl in the end Abe, but I'm jealous as hell she ain't me."

"Kary."

"Enough Abe, when I waited for you to walk through that door last night, I was ready to give up everything. Nothing else mattered. I don't have to have all this. I thought, all I have to have is you. But you made up your mind. Let me go live out the consequences in peace. I took a chance and followed my heart. I mailed a letter home telling my mother. For me, it's you, and I didn't give a damn about anything else. Without you no other future matters. There is no greater security than love found and returned. I followed my heart and it led me right here to this moment. So I guess this is where it was meant to be. Knowing that I did, at least once in this lifetime has to be enough."

"But Kary, there is more."

"Oh God Abe, stop with the knife twisting. Don't give me some line about someone out there for me, blah, blah, blah. Abe, I can't." Tears begin to roll down her face as she pulled her hands away to attempt to dry her eyes.

"I can't either. I can't watch you cry and go on and on. When I really just want to say shut the fuck up and let me talk. I can't stand here with you believing that just following your heart with no follow through is enough. That it is something wrong with your heart leading you right here to this moment. I can't stand here one second longer without telling you that I followed my heart right through that door and prayed it would land me right here." I touched her heart with my finger tip, leaned my forehead against hers and smiled my way into a warm soft kiss, "Kary Parsons, I love you too."

Yes, one man's enough is another's too much. My Kary Parsons would have been way too much for Buford Klaus Remington III. Later I told Kary that my time with Madeline showed me that it was just a moment. And one moment is not enough. I knew when I had held Kary in my lap in the villa, that one moment was not us. I knew also, I would never forget Madeline, lest I lose my breadth of measurement.

Kary and I headed decided to leave Cornerstone that evening. We took one final walk on the beach in remembrance of our time well spent. We saw Jai and Mortimer on the pier and stopped to say our farewell.

"Alright, Alright, Alright." Mortimer and Jai said in unison, big wide grins on their faces.

"Oh, you two," Kary said shyly as she pulled me close to her side.

"When are you leaving Jai?" She asked. "Well," Jai looked over at Mortimer "I think we're going to hang out here for the last big show."

"We?" I looked questioningly at Mortimer.

"Yeah, you know." He shrugged in Jai's direction. We all busted out laughing, now who didn't see this coming.

Kary and I wished them both luck and she gave hugs all around. I gave Mortimer a tight hug and promised to keep in touch.

I walked towards Jai, and then took a step back, "Well, since you gently inferred the half bow was slightly culturally offensive, and a firm handshake might be too gender qualifying, and a kiss on the hand, well you know…oh to hell with it." I pulled her close, tilted her fedora up just above her eyes, and firmly kissed her everso on the lips. Half turning, half spinning in retreat, fully expecting to be knocked the fuck out in epic proportions, a monumental blow, I was startled when instead she grabbed me hard and planted one firmly right back. As I stood in utter shock and disbelief, she pushed me back, affirmingly reset the fedora, tipped a good bye tug in our direction, and flashed a close contender for the million dollar grin. We watched them walk back down the pier towards Cornerstone.

Kary smiled and said, "I wonder if he'll ever get to do more than hold her hand." I just grinned. It is after all a Gentleman's Game.

The harbor almost looked bare without home base looming over it, until a luxury sized yacht began to creep over the horizon.

Kary looked out from the pier, "Holy shit, I'd like to meet the fucker that owns that beast."

"Hey" I nudged her. "I thought you said none of that mattered anymore."

She tilted her eyes up at me, "I just said that to get into your pants." She giggled.

"Would you settle for taking a ride in my sailboat for now?"

"Sure. You know I'm just kidding though, right?"

"I know Kary Parsons, right." I chuckled and squeezed her hand. As we approached the small sailboat she glanced at the side. "You named your boat Bo-Bo. Wow Abe, a writer, really? We may have to rethink your vocation if we're to make any money."

"Well now see, let me explain." I helped her into the boat. "You see it's all part of a bigger picture. Well, let me start with a truth."

"As in Truth or Dare?"

"Nah, as in true story about a little boy with a long name born into a big family, who moved to a tiny island, and then a big city. Made a short name for himself and met a pretty girl who talked a lot, but who was more than enough for him. Long story short Kary Parsons Abe stands for Alexander Barnabe Eyota.

Her eyes widened, glistening with tiny karats of tears.

Yeah, those Eyota's, and that right there is the bigger picture. Meet Ya-Ya Bo-Bo; a little name for a very big yacht. Squeal, Squeak, Squawk! Followed by a definite one-two punch.

As we sailed off into the sunset…Yeah, that just happened. As we sailed off into the sunset, I asked "Well, if Eden Club NYC is really done, how you feel about setting up garden in the US Virgin Islands?"

"Us?"

"Us" I affirmed. She pulled me close with a soft warm kiss, and flashed me her biggest grin to date; a billion dollars, just-like-new.

Epilogue:

"You don't say."

"Yup, they found her floating in the bathtub; the still water slowly dripping over the sides."

"You know it is going to be hell renting that villa again, and one of the far end ones at that."

"Are you kidding me? An award winning, glamorous author, and a suspicious death. Honey, that's one the Showman couldn't make up if he tried."

That's what was nagging me as I sat on the upper deck of Ya Ya Bo-Bo while Kary slept below. How did that damn scooter get back to Madeline's?

To Weave a Great Tale:

When you finally, momentarily silence the demons in your

head, you find that there's really nothing else going on.

So you rouse the dastardly beasts again,

just for someone to talk to.

Bloom-

1942 – 1972

Dezera R.B. Davis ©2015 All Rights Reserved

Made in the USA
Middletown, DE
29 February 2016